Christmas 2000

THE
PORTER ROCKWELL
CHRONICLES
VOL. 2

OTHER BOOKS BY THE AUTHOR:
Porter Rockwell: A Biography (1986)
Rockwell: U.S. Marshal, A Novel (1987)
The Porter Rockwell Chronicles, Vol. 1 (1999)

Richard Lloyd Dewey

THE
PORTER ROCKWELL
CHRONICLES

Vol. 2

STRATFORD
BOOKS

The Porter Rockwell Chronicles
Vol. 2

Book Cover Painting: Dan Thornton

Book Cover Design: Vance Hawkins

Photographic Essay Layout: Vance Hawkins

ISBN: 0-9616024-7-3
The Porter Rockwell Chronicles, Vol. 2

Stratford Books, L.C.
Eastern States Office
4308 37th Road North
Arlington, Virginia 22207

Stratford Books, L.C.
Western States Office
P.O. Box 1371
Provo, UT 84603-1371

First Printing: December, 2000

This book is printed on acid-free paper.

Printed in the United States of America

Nauvoo, Illinois, mid-1840s
by Dan Thornton

**Limited edition, signed and numbered art
prints of this painting are available in color
from the publisher. Please see Page 453.**

To Jacob Hyde Dewey,
Christian Miles Dewey,
Gabriel Lloyd Dewey,
and Julia Michele Dewey,
my next treasures.

FOREWORD

This volume is a continuation of the account of Porter Rockwell's life, a story that began in New York where Joseph Smith was Porter's best childhood friend. The story is told with historical accuracy in fictional form. It is also an early history of the Church of Jesus Christ of Latter-day Saints.

PREFACE

In May 1839 the saints launched another exodus. Their destination — Commerce, Illinois. The area holds a fascinating history to many observers:

Joseph had purchased the land from one Isaac Galland, who had settled his own family in Iowa across the Mississippi River from Commerce in 1829. That same year, the federal government had granted the Sac and Fox Native American tribes almost 200,000 acres. Five years later, Galland and other land speculators had begun buying land in the area, including the tract owned by the Sac and Fox tribes.

In 1839 Galland moved to Commerce. Soon he met Israel Barlow, one of the "saints" (members of the Church of Jesus Christ of Latter-day Saints) who had fled to Iowa from Far West. From that meeting Joseph would buy hundreds of acres at Commerce on excellent terms.

Meanwhile, when the saints had fled to Quincy, Illinois, its county — Adams — was one of the most populous counties in the state. Coincidentally, when the saints of Kirtland, Ohio had years earlier fled to Far West, Missouri they had crossed the Mississippi River at Quincy.

Upon Joseph's release from his captors and his arrival at Quincy in early spring of 1839, the prospects had looked good for staying in Quincy, but Joseph felt they should build their own city away from populated areas. So when Commerce became available, he jumped at the chance.

In addition to Commerce, they would settle across the river in Iowa. Four months before the May exodus, in January 1839, Brigham Young had led 400 saints to both Illinois and Iowa, with the Iowa saints establishing themselves at Fort Des Moines. Brigham — and fellow future church presidents John Taylor and Wilford Woodruff — lived at the fort after fleeing Missouri, living in vacant army barracks. The fort had been built five years previously by the War Department, but in 1837 the army had abandoned it when more whites settled the area. Brigham soon began talks with Galland about buying the barracks along with two parcels of land across the river from each other — Commerce and Montrose/Fort Des Moines. Joseph stepped in and concluded negotiations.

They bought about 20,000 acres in Iowa, including parts of Keokuk, Montrose, and the town of Nashville. They also secured land in Lee County, Iowa. They were able to purchase it by issuing "Half Breed Land Company" stock. At least 13 communities were soon settled in Iowa by the saints, with the town of Zarahemla the most populous. (Zarahemla alone would claim 326 members by 1841.) But the *Illinois* communities they would settle, of course, would become the most population intensive.

Both the Iowa and Illinois acreage Joseph targeted had enjoyed steady growth in the 1820's. The third and fourth towns of substantial Mormon population would be Lima in Adams County, Illinois near Quincy, and Ramus in Hancock County, Illinois, closer to their chief headquartering city at Commerce.

However, Joseph and other leaders wished to keep most of their people closer to Commerce in order to help build the temple. Commerce's indigenous population of several dozen families was spread along the Mississippi River about 1 $1/2$ miles, before Joseph's people moved there.

Thus, the saints settled both sides of the Mississippi River, with farms expanding beyond the original plat map.

The area's earliest roots extend back to 1674. Two tribes, the Sac and Fox, settled in nearby trading posts and small villages along the river banks of the Mississippi. They lived on corn, rice, melons, wild grapes and game — including buffalo, deer and turkey — along with river fish.

Throughout the 1700's white settlers moved in — mostly French. In the autumn of 1779 Americans had begun settling the area, mostly families from Tennessee and Kentucky. Then in 1800 the whites had begun pouring in. By 1810 Illinois had 12,282 official inhabitants. 10 years later it had quadrupled to 55,221. Before 1839 when the saints arrived, settlers had poured into towns all along the Mississippi River in addition to Commerce.

Meanwhile, the village at Commerce had been called Quashquema, also settled by the Sac and Fox, which initially were two separate tribes living side by side. But in 1805 they merged. They also settled a village across the river near the future Montrose, Iowa on other acres the saints would procure. By 1826 almost 500 tribe members inhabited the Commerce settlement, but throughout the 1820's they were forced from all their villages.

That action precipitated the Black Hawk War of 1832 when they and other Native Americans returned to the state to resettle their original lands; however, the whites had by now completely taken dominion over the land, and had power in numbers to stay off most attacks. It was an exciting time, to say the least, for white settlers pushing the borders of the frontier.

Other interesting tidbits:

Twenty-one years before the saints settled Illinois, it had achieved statehood as the 21st state on December 3, 1818.

With regards to its white settlement history, Commerce was indeed the "frontier" of the state: it was 250 miles southwest of Chicago and 185 miles north of St. Louis.

After Quashquema, the settlement was next called Venus, settled by one James White, a man who had purchased it from the Sac and Fox tribes for 200 bags of corn. The "Trading Oak" in Nauvoo marked the spot where that first transaction had occurred, and White's family was the first group of permanent white settlers there.

In 1829 when Hancock County was organized, Venus was actually the first county seat, and established a post office. By the next year Venus had two dozen families which the post office served. Later, before Joseph's people settled there, the county seat moved to Carthage, closer to the center of the county.

Within four years Venus grew to a hundred white settlers. It was then surveyed and renamed Commerce in 1834 by two settlers — Alexander White and Joseph Teas.

When the saints arrived in 1839, several stores were actually operating. The first two in the area were owned by men who would soon convert to the faith: Hiram Kimball and Amos Davis.

As for Hancock County, Joseph planned 18 communities with Commerce being "the hub of the wheel." Joseph quickly renamed Commerce to "Nauvoo," which meant "the City Beautiful," its root in a Hebrew word. While it quickly became a city of extraordinary beauty, it was a very difficult wilderness when they first moved in: Swamps, thickets and heavy woods literally prevented travel from the river to the east side of town.

Before and during this period the saints attempted to convert Native Americans. Some joined them and moved to Nauvoo, including the Sac-Fox and Potawatomi tribespeople.

The Nauvoo High Council immediately obtained control of the ferryboat which ran between Montrose and Nauvoo, since the river divided the two main settlements of the saints. But Porter was not included in its operation because the pay, one must assume, was too low to support married men with families. He could better serve his family and his parents by working the farmland designated for the saints east of Nauvoo, which was actually soil the Sac-Fox tribe had farmed.

Within months after their May 1839 move, nearly every family became sick, including Porter's. The culprit – malaria, encountered from the swamps in the city. They were also still weak from physical and emotional exhaustion created by the exodus from Far West. Joseph Smith, Brigham Young and others gave priesthood blessings to many of the ill on both sides of the river, where many were healed. Nevertheless, numerous others died during this period from not only malaria, but fevers and measles — especially large numbers of children.

The booming town with all its construction — this time of superior, large houses and buildings, compared to the small huts and cabins in all their previous communities — was a source of soaring morale among the saints on one hand, while a trial by disease on the other.

Under Joseph Smith's supervision, two hundred and fifty structures went up immediately, with several hundred more within the year. Joseph's primary task was to drain all the water from the swamps, which he successfully engineered with the aid of associates skilled in large-plan irrigation, and then with further consultation he laid out the street plans for the township.

The city design was based on a plat laid out for Jackson County, Missouri known as "City of Zion," but the city blocks were smaller. Each consisted of four acres, and every family was given one acre on which to build their home. By 1841 nearly 80 percent of the original Nauvoo plat was in use. After a required number of people were ready to move in, new streets would be surveyed and "opened." So, the town was actually planned out in 1839 before it was inhabited — a revolutionary concept for the day of which the citizens were proud. The first city plan had been papered out on August 30, 1839, at which time the church owned 671 acres. Interestingly, even after Nauvoo was inhabited, it would take almost two years to officially organize the place. On February 3, 1841 the city would finally be certified by the state.

The town council, autonomous of but obviously influenced by Joseph, had immediately gone to work at their meeting place

— the Red Brick Store — of beautifying the city, launching public works projects, and passing laws on building restrictions.

Due to low funding, many new building projects were slow to be completed, including new streets as well as road repairs. But for Joseph it was a good problem: The place was crawling with converts aplenty.

The post office was in Sidney Rigdon's kitchen, against the wall in a corner.

Joseph's people began prospering faster than they had ever dreamed. Near the ferry landing up the hill, but still near the river, Joseph moved into his first Nauvoo home, and added onto it. There, he would enjoy a view of the river to calm his soul on the distressing days that lay ahead, and there he would receive many a visit from his close, personal, childhood friend, Orin Porter Rockwell . . .

CHAPTER 1

The clean streets and well-landscaped, superbly designed lay-out of the city won for the Saints high praise, but Porter was not happy. He was mired in manual labor that bored him to extinction.

In the late spring of 1839 his cabin was completed but his parents were forced to live with them because their parents' property, several hundred yards away, was in swampland.

Porter therefore set out with his father each day after sunrise to help build his parents' house. Orin seemed to be weakening daily. Luana felt she was going insane with the elder Rockwell couple living right in her home. Particularly with Porter's mother.

She said nothing, however, to Porter or anyone about it.

For food, he attended his backyard garden and his plot of farm land east of the city. This occupied most of his time when he was not building his parents' house.

He spent, predictably, certain amounts of his free time with Joseph, and usually took Emily and occasionally Caroline with him to visit his childhood friend.

While his visits with Joseph were frequent, they were of short duration. The prophet greeted him with excitement and they always hugged, but their meetings were generally interrupted by affairs of the city and church. Porter had always regarded him as his intellectual superior yet felt comfortable in his presence. He was in fact amazed at how Joseph had always made him and others feel that way. Except for Joseph, Porter felt at best only tolerated among the Rigdon/intellectual contingency of the church leadership. Among other leaders, by contrast, he felt held in high esteem.

Joseph often confided in him of family matters, and Porter was always charmed by the candor of his friend and his openness. Knowing Porter was not inclined to volunteer advice — unlike Rigdon and some others in his circle — the prophet particularly enjoyed his relationship with this old friend, almost as he would with a loyal little brother. Their roles since childhood had not changed.

When Porter would report to Luana of their visits, he would amplify few details, only a passing comment about how good Joseph's health was and on the growth of the city.

Ugly was meanwhile appreciating the new territory more than Porter had ever expected. He seemed to lie around in the sun less than usual: He'd sojourn into the bog, days at a time, and live off the rich wildlife, finding ecstasy in the sulfur-laden swamp water that brewed new forms of dead marsh carcasses in which he could delightfully roll. He loved this place like no other on earth.

Porter meanwhile received from Joseph extra ammunition to target practice.

Luana became annoyed with the gunshots each morning in the backyard, and one morning when she watched him shooting, a new thought occurred — he was becoming obsessed with this idiotic pistol. Soon, from his farm income, he secured a new rifle, and received from Joseph even more ammunition.

"I want you to pay extra close attention to my safety, Porter," Joseph finally told him one evening. "I've found Brother Shadrack Roundy and others willing, but I enjoy your companionship particularly, and the Missourians still have warrants out for my arrest — they'd drag me across the river any day they could, and lynch me. But they might have trouble trying that with you around. I'm not sure."

Porter smiled at him.

"So," said Joseph, "can you shoot as good as what I've heard?"

"See for yourself."

The two men walked into Joseph's backyard and Joseph placed glass containers on a fence. He stood beside Porter as his old friend fired four shots with four pistols and exploded four bottles.

Joseph smiled. "I think I do like having you around."

CHAPTER 2

It was now mid-summer of 1839. Porter had just turned 26. He strolled into his modest two-room cabin one afternoon with a basket full of tomatoes he'd picked. Caroline and Emily accompanied him.

Luana picked up a sharp knife and began slicing warm bread.

"Where have you been?" she said.

"Getting these." He plopped down the tomato basket.

"I mean before that."

"With my friend."

"Yeah, look at these tomatoes. Why couldn't you spend more time picking good ones?"

He knew what she really meant. "Well he needs me. Especially now."

"Why now?"

"He asked me to be his bodyguard."

"Why didn't you tell me about this earlier?"

"'Just found out."

"How much is he paying you?"

"'Isn't."

"So your services aren't worth anything?"

"Luana," he said, picking up a ripe tomato and biting into the luscious, juicy meat which squirted onto his shirt, "even if he had any money I wouldn't ask for it."

"Aren't you entitled to make a living? Can't we eat?"

He was surprised at her sudden outburst, and nodded to the basket:

"I don't see us starving."

"Others are prospering. They have cows, chickens, hogs, acres of wheat, corn; where's ours? Where's our cash money so I can buy a new knife-sharpening stone — and we still need cloth from the general store for new dresses for the girls."

"Luana, I work as hard as I can on the acres. And you know what I think of the acres."

"Yeah, well they feed us."

"Other work feeds folks too."

"Fine," she said. "I forgot how you're 'above' farm work. My father's a gentleman farmer — but I suppose you're above him. Even though he kept me well-supported."

"I'm sorry, but I thought the hours I work the fields keep you supported enough."

"Why do you have to define for me what is enough?" Don't I have a right to my own way of viewing what I need?"

"I just thought — "

"*You* thought?" she said.

"I think — "

"Let me do my own thinking, if you don't mind." She walked outside.

Porter followed behind her. "Honey, I really am trying to make you happy."

"Then earn as much as we need."

"I work the acres till I go crazy."

"It's not enough. Keep at them till past dark, if necessary, like other men."

"I'm not other men. Like you're not other women."

"You're right. Other men work as long as it takes, but you find yourself needing to go off to your old friend's place every night. And now as a 'bodyguard.'"

"It's only when he travels to the villages."

"Why can't others go with him?"

"So you don't want me to help him?"

"You can help whomever you want, but do it after you've given us what we need!"

"I'm sorry," he said, walking to the well and looking down it.

She stared at him a moment, then blew out a long, silent sigh. Having softened, she strolled up behind him. Her voice calmed. "You really don't think you'll ever like this work, do you?"

"I wish I did, but it drives me loco."

"Maybe you are loco," she smiled. "And maybe I'm loco for staying with you." He turned and she hugged him.

"There's got to be something you can do that you don't hate so much."

"I don't know, short of stealing a steamboat."

"The river's still in your blood?"

He nodded and stared off at the house across the street, one far nicer than his.

She asked about the ferry, but they both knew the local ferry operation owned by the city was out of the question. Still too little money.

"Maybe we can take turns working the acres," she said. "Do you think Joseph could help you find something?"

"You're not working the acres, honey. You stay here with the young 'uns the way the Lord wants it to be, and I'll see if I can't wrestle up a steamship line of my own," he said dryly.

She smiled.

"I reckon," he continued, "you're having a tough time with my folks living here."

"It's a lot deeper than you think," she said.

"Having two extra folks around can make a lot of work," he continued.

"One extra can make it difficult," she said.

He knew what she meant, sensing her personality conflict with his mother; so he purposely said nothing.

Despite her attempts at peacemaking with him, Luana was miffed that she was expected to continue putting up with his parents in her house. His silence was the worst answer she could possibly hear.

Porter continued helping his father build the largest house in his life. He wished for his parents to enjoy their last years on the soil; therefore, he put in twice the hours his father could. His younger brothers also aided them, but with less skills.

Luana was relieved when his parents finally moved out one late summer day into their new home. After aiding his mother into the large, wood-framed house Porter stood back and studied it proudly.

"You ever seen such a house, Mama?"

"Never in all my days, son. You've created a lovely home for us."

Porter beamed.

"I would that you could be so proud of our home," said Luana over dinner that night. Porter disregarded her criticism and spent several minutes explaining the intricacies and vastness of the construction project, detailing the finishing touches he still needed to add. Then he pondered aloud:

"We'll have such a home someday. They're old and deserve it now while they're still alive."

Luana wondered why she could not have such a house now. After all, she'd put up with tremendous trials, had borne him two children and raised them for him, and here he was building a beautiful home for his parents. She chewed her cornbread more firmly than usual.

CHAPTER 3

When Porter returned the next afternoon from a visit with Joseph, Luana was concerned over her husband's newest report — that he had committed to help drain the land through all the city, along with dozens of other volunteers, for the civic and church buildings and for the widows and arriving settlers who had no time or ability to either build a home or drain the water from their land — yet he would not finish repairing the gate on their own property. Luana said nothing, and could not quite bring herself to giving him much attention, which in turn irked him. She stewed over the problem with sleepless nights. To top it off, she was pregnant again, due in October. The fact Porter would not help much with domestic chores — just as he had not assisted much during her previous two pregnancies — caused her further consternation.

In the home where Porter was raised, his father had stuck to the farm chores and his mother to the domestic duties, pregnancy or no pregnancy. There was no time to alter their lifestyles, although Orin had pitched in when precious few minutes were available after the day's farming before he would collapse exhausted into bed. Porter now followed the same tradition. He helped Luana whenever he could during her pregnancy but, to her, his effort was negligible compared to her needs and what she was used to seeing while growing up.

Meanwhile, thousands of European Mormon converts poured in. Additionally, some from local Illinois congregations began embracing the faith of the Church of Jesus Christ of Latter-day Saints. Consequently, some rumbling erupted among concerned, local ministers. Additionally, political entities opposed to Mormon thinking became concerned by the numbers of converts. Porter, meanwhile, met few of these converts except those most closely associated with Joseph, as he primarily performed the arduous tasks of digging and shoveling.

Luana was pleased the day he announced he had finished his swamp-drainage work for the city projects. Later that afternoon they took a stroll, and just before sunset sauntered across the hill rising in the center of the city. They viewed the landscaped city streets, houses, and distant dales. It was on this hill at sunset that she announced she was trying her hardest to be a good wife. Despite his faults, she would try her best to overlook them, she said, and now asked him what she could do to be a better wife.

"Nothing," he smiled. "You're just fine." In reality he was still reeling from the verbal blows he'd absorbed over the years of marriage, but what good would it do to dredge up old river sludge? He forgave on a daily basis, yet was still wounded.

Together they walked back to their home on a warm twilight wind. It was early September 1839.

A certain peace descended over Porter, and as they walked he felt a security with his life he had never before felt. He was somewhat surprised then, upon reaching his parents' home to gather their children, that Luana would suddenly announce:

"This is only so permanent as you desire to make it."

When they arrived at their own home and placed their sleeping children in bed, he took Luana in his arms and caressed the hair away from her green eyes. Despite the hurt he felt from her comment minutes earlier, he pushed it aside and said:

"Not much seems left for me to do but till the land. And to love you."

And that's all he said that night.

She decided to be optimistic, and took condolence in his words. Then she studied him carefully over the next week and, with compassion, perceived his ever-growing frustration with mere farm work.

However, it soon reached apparently undefinable proportions and created a new problem with which she did not know how to deal:

Once he had completed both his parents' home and the city drainage projects, he quickly became less productive: He cut his farm hours in half then, after a short visit with Joseph each night, would make his way to Rockwell clan gatherings at his parents' home. There, he would find relief from farm work by making himself the center of attention and telling outrageous stories to make his relatives and neighbors roar. Liquor would be passed around. Although Emma Smith was a proponent of complete abstinence, Joseph saw nothing wrong with good, solid merriment, at least during these years. However, Porter still drank sparingly, just enough to loosen his spirits. Once, Luana went to retrieve him at 2 A.M. from his father's home and found a dozen men cawing and jeckling. She decided not to enter. At 4 A.M. he returned home, dancing a jig.

Luana thought of confronting him for his lack of work ethic, but was too upset with his recent evening behavior to even know where to begin.

She ignored the problem altogether.

Then she began internalizing his behavior, directing it towards herself, taking the blame, and forgetting her earlier, accurate impressions that he was indeed just frustrated with far more than her.

Cooler winds stirred.

At a nearby Nauvoo general store, Luana and Porter gathered necessities which they could little afford because all their previous equity had been put into the farm at Far West, and this year's crops could not be harvested until autumn, so they bought what objects they could with their last silver coins.

Before leaving, they saw three families trudging past in their wagons outside, obviously worn and hungered. Luana did not even know these people, but could not take her eyes from them. The street was quiet except for two crying babies which two of the women carried. Luana and Porter stepped outside to greet them. They had just arrived from the East. Luana suddenly handed each of the women all the drygoods she had moments earlier purchased at the store. Porter made no attempt to stop her. He was proud of her. As the families wheeled away in their creaking wagons, he placed his hand on her side and squeezed her closer to him. They watched the families roll down Water Street toward Joseph's house to learn where they should go next.

CHAPTER 4

The next morning Porter arose before Luana awakened. When she came to consciousness she discovered him dressing Emily. She sat up in bed.

"What're you doing?"

"Taking Emily with me."

"Where?"

"Joseph is going on an overnight trip."

Groggily she responded, "What're you talking about?"

"He's going to visit some of our people in the villages."

"And you think you're taking Emily again?"

"She wants to go."

"No, Porter. If Joseph needs a bodyguard, you're obviously engaged in dangerous business."

"We'll be safe."

"It is no place for Emily."

"Her place is with me if she wants to go."

"You will leave her home with me."

"I'm taking her." At that, Porter led Emily outside and helped her up to his saddle, where they rode off together.

Luana stood at the doorway, shocked. "What on earth do you think you're doing, Porter?"

"Bye, Mama," said Emily.

Luana stared as Porter and Emily rode away. This time she could not cry. She had never felt so lonely . . . and cold . . . towards her husband . . . nor towards life.

Porter and Emily rode beside Joseph, heading to Morley's Settlement. On country roads Joseph felt especially vulnerable, so Porter's company made not only the hours go faster but, seeing his gruff friend's several loaded weapons, Joseph felt he was under the protection of a veritable armada.

"One thing I hope," said Joseph, "is that Luana is handling this all right."

Porter said nothing.

"That's the one thing I appreciate about Emma. I know you're not as close to my wife as you could be, but she is a wonderful support to all I do. She has put up with numerous trials. That's one thing we can say about our companions, isn't it, Porter?"

Porter grunted.

Lying beside a campfire on their return trip, Emily slept with her head on Porter's chest.

The autumn leaves were floating to the woodland floor, and Porter enjoyed the brisk odor of the air. He sat stroking Emily's forehead.

Joseph faced him, sitting across the fire. "I'll never forget those days in Manchester."

"I'll never forget you saving me from those bullies," said Porter.

"What bullies?"

"I reckon you've seen so many of 'em it's hard to remember which are which."

"Those are men I feel sorry for," said Joseph. "They feel a sense of power over others, have usually been abused themselves, and know no other way of treating others. I truly feel badly for bullies of all sorts."

"They only make me mad as a hornet."

"I know how you feel."

Porter appreciated that as charitable as Joseph was, he never gave him a feeling of judging or condemnation. He knew Joseph was right, but just did not have it in him to accept those who persecuted him.

Emily awakened and with eyes half-opened became interested in what the two were discussing.

"Some of our biggest enemies have later embraced us," explained Joseph. "That's why I personally pray for our enemies. It's never too late to repent and accept the Restored Gospel, no matter how bitter or antagonistic they may have been. Even some who were once among us in Missouri and later dissented — then went to the local mobs and riled them up against us — even some of them returned to our fold."

"You've been betrayed by every kind, huh?" said Porter.

"I know one kind who never will."

Porter regarded him curiously. From Joseph's gaze he knew Joseph meant him. "But there will always be a temptation which, when not dealt with, could become a soul's Achilles' heal," said Joseph.

Porter's eyes lowered, not certain what that might be but, fearful that Joseph always seemed to be right about such matters, he hoped to simply be found on the right side of things when the deck was reshuffled and everything was divied up. No matter which temptations might arise to distract him in the meantime.

Emily gazed up at her father and smiled. "I just hope we can always live by each other."

Joseph's eyes floated softly down to her.

She studied Joseph's big blue eyes. "Pa, I want all our family and friends to live in heaven together."

"I reckon if we get along here," said Porter, "that's just what'll happen."

"You think Mama and you can get along someday?"

Porter peered down at her, surprised. He felt a certain anguish that his daughter perceived the problems between him and Luana. It had never occurred to him his daughter listened to their conflicts, or that the disagreements had to any degree concerned her.

"I reckon we'll all be happier if we try harder," said Porter.

"That's usually what it takes," added Joseph. "Trying."

But Porter was not prepared for the actual war that would soon surface between him and Luana. In the meantime he,

Emily and Joseph arrived the next morning at Nauvoo. Joseph turned down a different street to his home while Porter and Emily rode to his parents. It was late September 1839.

Upon entering the house, Porter was taken back by Orin's dramatically degenerating condition. His cough was much worse now as he sat by the fire.

"Papa . . . "

"Just don't fuss over me," said Orin.

"He made it worse," complained Sarah. "He had to go out and act like a 17 year old, chopping firewood in the cold."

"You worry about yourself, Old Ma," snapped Orin.

"You gotta take care of yourself, Pa," said Porter.

Emily hugged her grandfather. "You'll be all right, won't you, Grandpa?"

"Yeah, I'll be all right." He picked up Emily and placed her on his lap, then kissed her on the cheek.

"Porter," said Sarah, "you think you could help out by finishing that cord of firewood? After that we need our crops harvested at the acres. I hate to ask that of you, son, but we can't let the crops go to waste, and we need food for the winter."

"I'll be glad to, Ma." Porter indeed was. Nothing was ever spoken or implied about the bad ferry debt, where Porter had spent his parents' savings and repaid them only a fraction before their expulsion from Jackson County, but his conscience now directed him to help his parents in any manner possible, no matter the cost of time or effort. And all concerned knew he had more than re-imbursed them by building their house. Hard-cost-wise it had been paid for with only a few dollars, the lumber having been rafted down the river from Wisconsin, while

Porter had pitched in a couple dollars he'd earned from help-ing others, much to Luana's consternation. The day before, however, Orin had attempted to off-set her feelings with a unique gift of appreciation.

Outside, Luana was arriving, searching for Emily. She had heard from Joseph that they had returned to town, and she wanted her daughter back at the cabin. From outside, she over-heard Sarah's request to Porter for more labor, and quickly entered the open front door.

"Luana!" said Sarah cheerfully.

Luana ignored all but Porter, walking towards him and panting with anger. "So you can just take on more fences to paint while the paint itself gets even thinner?"

Porter was stunned by Luana's abrupt attack in front of his whole family. He was also angered by it:

"I am not going to refuse helping my parents, Luana."

"You think I'm asking that?" she said. "Why can't we get some-thing organized, and get neighbors and your brothers to help? Why does it always have to be you for things to fall upon?"

Sarah cut in, "Luana, I'm so sorry if I've intruded on some-thing with you."

"It's not me I'm worried about," said Luana. "She walked to the doorway and glared back at him. "It's if the paint is even worth using."

That night at their cabin Porter lay sleeping beside Emily, who often slept between him and Luana. Someone rapped at the door.

Not wishing to disturb his sleeping family, Porter moved quickly out of bed to answer it. Standing there was his brother Horace.

"It's Pa. Come quick."

CHAPTER 5

Porter grabbed Emily and took her with him to his parents'. He felt a lump in his gut, fearful of the worse. He entered his folks' foyer and went straight to their bedroom. He saw his father in bed and knelt at his side. Emily ran to him and hugged him. Orin hugged back, but with failing strength.

"I think I'm heading down the road, honey."

Emily, knowing what he meant, began to sob. She had determined on the way there not to shed tears, but could not refrain.

"Son," said Orin, "I've spoken to your brothers and sisters already, but I haven't talked to you. First off, I don't like these maudlin farewells, so let's get that out in the open," he smiled.

"I think you'll fight this all right," said Porter, his eyes glistening.

"I'll try," he said softly, "but I think it's time. He thought a moment and his throat tightened. "One thing I've gotta say. I want you to forget about something."

Porter stared at him curiously.

"When you were growing up, you were a little boy with big eyes wanting to be picked up and held. But I see myself pushing you away so I could go back to the field. Farming them extra hours for extra cash was so all-fired important. Now, it ain't. At least not as much as the few seconds it would've taken to hold you up and give you a squeeze."

"I don't remember that too well," said Porter, trying to comfort him but recalling the memory.

"My ma," explained Orin, "says Pa did the same to me. I am so sorry. 'Cause at night I would look at you and feel like the luckiest man alive. But you needed me in your life while you was awake, and I didn't give that to you."

Porter's tears flowed down his cheeks. He finally stated his heart's deepest feelings. "Please — don't go, Pa."

"'Not sure I've got the choice, son. But I'll tell you what," he said, trying again for levity to ease the moment, "If some soul named Gabriel or something comes my way and asks me if I want to follow him, I'll tell him to go jump in the Lake."

"I'll get them," said Porter seriously.

"Get who?"

"The folks who did this."

"You leave them alone," said Orin. "You've done enough skunk-kicking in your day."

"Even if it's their fault?" muttered Porter. "They shouldn't pay for it?"

"Nobody's at fault here. I'm only sick."

Porter's mother blurted out, "Emily, tell your grandpa he's just an ornery old man."

"She's right," said Orin to Emily. "I just want some attention, I guess. And I *am* an ornery old cuss."

Porter gazed upon him, certain the exposure forced upon him from the exodus to Clay County, and later to Illinois, was the reason for his father's collapsing health.

"Yeah, I guess you're right," said Porter. "Who needs to kick a skunk?"

"I taught you as a kid," said Orin, "when you kick a skunk, nobody wins."

Yet deep down Porter knew full well he would have his revenge.

At the sunshine-laden funeral, Porter heard not one word of the bishop's eulogy. All he could hear were the sounds of the rolling, turbulent Missouri River when, drenched by rain upon the river bank, his father had caught consumption.

Porter fought his tears watching both his mother and Emily crying. He figured at that moment the hardest things about a parent passing on were unresolved feelings. Even though his father had apologized for neglecting him while growing up, he was not ready before his father's death to confess his own tender feelings. But he was certain of one fact. He truly missed his pa, and wished he had one more day with him to say how much he loved him.

Luana was also tearful, feeling an affection for the kindly old farmer who had sacrificed far more than what she could for Porter. She felt guilty for all the times she had fought to keep father and son apart, but pushed away the feelings. Turning from the grave, she strolled with Porter and the two girls toward their home as the funeral gathering dispersed. Hearing Emily sob, she caressed her daughter's back, hoping to in some measure provide comfort.

After they had walked fifty feet, Porter knelt to one knee and hugged Emily. "Let's walk back and see Grandpa one last time," he said.

Luana watched as Emily and Porter strode back to the grave and looked down. Porter gave a short little salute. Emily watched him and, holding back sobs, also saluted. She tried to be brave, and squeezing her father's hand hard she mustered the courage to say, with a clear, tearless voice that would make even Orin proud, "Bye, ornery old cuss."

CHAPTER 6

A month later on October 26, 1839 Porter's first son was born: Orrin DeWitt. While Porter waited as before — with his mother acting as mid-wife and neighbors assisting — his duties were limited, as always, to bringing in the hot water, then waiting outside the cabin until he heard the baby's wail, whereupon the child would be brought out for him to hold. He was used to this system, although now felt emptier without his father joining him. Little Emily, now six and three-quarters, sat down beside him. She had heard from her aunts that she could "replace" Porter's father out on the porch and, for Porter to a big extent, it worked. The baby, Orrin DeWitt, looked just like his grandpa Orin, so much so that it caused Porter to find a tear in his own eye. The wonder each child brought was marvelling to him.

Porter tilled the land the next afternoon. He suddenly dropped the reins and stared at the sun. His life seemed increasingly useless. He sauntered to the cabin depressed. Luana had nothing to say as she nursed the day-old baby.

He went to see Joseph. It was their first visit in three weeks.

"Come in, Porter, have dinner with us."

Porter joined them and afterwards sat in Joseph's study at the Homestead, listening intently to his every word.

"Poverty is hurting us more than anything," said Joseph, "despite our prosperous house-building. Too many families were done in by the Missouri Wars. I've decided to appeal to the national government for redress. Porter, I'm leaving tomorrow for Washington. I want you to join me."

Porter felt a thrill inside him, yet was reserved. Joseph knew the problem and smiled on him with short advice, "The Lord will provide. Family and friends will come to her aid with necessities and food while you're gone. Trust Him."

Porter walked toward home feeling doubtful yet hopeful. He felt only he could protect the prophet if the prophet needed protecting. He felt a remarkable confidence in himself growing in that regard. Three others would be going on the journey with them, he learned, but he knew he would be Joseph's only guardian. He glanced at the stars and found a brighter twinkle in them. He seemed for an instant to see beyond them, to other stars, even brighter, and the effect was mesmerizing. He glanced down. He knew he should go. His house was a half mile away, and as he approached it he stepped up his gait.

Luana was inside, displeased at his returning so late.

As he held his infant son he suddenly wished the Washington journey would be cancelled. All excitement he had felt for the trip was now transferred to this precious child. Furthermore, he discovered the task of making the announcement of the Washington trip to his wife thoroughly distasteful. He began by clearing his throat, then explaining Joseph's admonition to them to trust in the Lord; finally, he told her of the journey with Joseph, and informed her he had visited his mother and sisters already and had arranged for his family's care.

The waves of disbelief Luana felt were almost a shock. After midnight she developed a fever.

The next afternoon it subsided, but when Porter attempted explaining the journey further she got so incensed that she asked him to leave the cabin.

By the next morning — October 29, 1839, two days after the baby was born — he made final preparations to leave, but felt a deep remorse. Emily's sobs tore at his soul as he backed away. Luana refused to look at him.

However, as he went out the door, she called him back and gave him a kiss on the cheek. He did not see the torment in her eyes as he left, but he did feel a storm of heartache over leaving the infant and the two girls as he climbed onto his newly acquired carriage. It especially hurt seeing Emily's confused face. The vehicle had been given to Porter by his father before he died, for the countless hours he had spent building for him, despite his loan that was lost in the barge business at Big Blue. The carriage was a possession Orin Rockwell had enjoyed for the year he had owned it. He had made the gift as a strategic peacemaking move, sensing a rift growing between his son and Luana. The carriage was also a thank-you gift for having helped them so many weeks; additionally, he figured Luana would downright enjoy the contraption.

Luana could not care less about the carriage, but she did appreciate her father-in-law's concern. She had kissed him on the cheek for the gift.

Now arriving at the Homestead, Porter discovered Joseph in his characteristic, bright cheer; Joseph hugged and kissed each of his own children and Emma goodbye, and they all waved as Joseph, Elias Higbee, Sidney Rigdon and Dr. Robert Foster climbed into the carriage and rolled down the road with Porter at the helm.

Porter's heart was the lowest he had ever felt it. He felt justified to make the journey, but the haunting image of his children's expressions were stamped upon his mind and he could not shake them loose, no matter how hard he tried.

CHAPTER 7

The hours passed as days, and by the week's end Porter felt he'd been gone on his trip for a year. Through the second week he had sleepless nights. The realization hit him he had spent too many hours in his life away from the little ones.

By the time they reached Ohio he was feeling an appreciation for Luana he had not before felt. This would be their longest parting yet, and when he began recalling her recent coolness, his heart quaked inside.

He said little to his companions. His mind was twirling on past images like an obsession.

In Ohio, when they stopped at an inn for food and refreshment, Robert Foster flirted with a bar maid and began caressing her inappropriately. Joseph was stunned, the others humiliated, and Porter amused with the man — a pompous, self-proclaimed leader with an appetite for chubby, loose women. Porter did not like Foster that much, nor the high-nosed Rigdon, both of whom perceived him as a lower-class creature.

It was therefore not with a great deal of pleasure that when Rigdon took ill in Ohio, Porter and Foster were the ones asked to remain behind. Joseph Smith and Elias Higbee transferred to a different coach and continued their journey to the District of Columbia.

After several days Rigdon felt well enough to resume their journey, and Porter was relieved to again enjoy his freedom from distasteful, snobbish self-proclaimed gentlemen as he drove his carriage, while Rigdon and Foster were forced to remain caged in the back.

"How come you're going so fast!" shouted Rigdon.

"This thing bounces like a box," criticized Foster.

Porter snapped the reigns as he saw larger rocks looming in the road ahead, and smiled.

He could not wait to be rid of them. He smiled at images of them bouncing out the windows. "I lost them, Joseph," he fantasized saying to him later. "They just disappeared in thin air. Somewhere in Ohio."

The men howled and moaned at Porter's inept driving as they bounced around inside the cabin.

"Inept?" replied Porter to them softly. "Nay, my brethren, that took great skill."

They finally split up in southern Pennsylvania. There, Rigdon and Foster stayed with Rigdon's brother, while Porter felt greatly relieved to proceed alone to Washington. Outside the city he caught up to Joseph and Higbee.

"Where's Brother Rigdon?" said Joseph.

"Recuperating at his brother's place. Still sick. And a bit bruised I might add."

"What?"

"It's these long hard trips," said Porter with a twinkle.

Joseph held a serious expression. "You couldn't wait for him?"

"You couldn't have paid me to." He finally caught Joseph holding back a smile. All three men spent most of November 28, 1839 searching for the cheapest boarding house in Washington.

The next morning at the designated hour of appointment, Porter and Higbee escorted Joseph to the White House to meet the President of the United States.

Porter waited impatiently outside the President's office.

Joseph Smith and Elias Higbee meanwhile met with President Martin Van Buren. Porter had shaken hands with the President upon arrival, and frankly had found him as pompous a goat as Rigdon and Foster. 'They oughta all ride off in the sunset together,' smiled Porter to himself. 'Over a cliff. I'll donate the carriage.'

When the prophet emerged from his fifteen-minute meeting with the President, his countenance was appreciably fallen. Porter knew the outcome. Joseph explained the meeting verbatim to Porter on their walk from the White House to the hotel. "Gentlemen," the President had said, "your cause is just, but I can do nothing for you. If I take up for you I shall lose the vote of Missouri."

Porter was incensed. His thoughts of his children and Luana ceased for a few minutes. He asked Joseph what they could do.

"Take our issue to Congress. That's why Congress is here."

Porter and Joseph returned to their room. There, Joseph related his experience to the other Mormons gathered.

The following day Porter and Joseph went to Congress. Joseph spoke with a committee chairman and learned they needed one thing — the testimonies of those who had lost their property in the Missouri persecutions.

At their boarding room Joseph composed a letter to the church's High Council in Nauvoo, requesting affidavits to be gathered from the injured and sent to him in a single package.

Christmas season came to Washington, and Porter missed his family doubly. He worried incessantly over the children and Luana. Joseph then left for Philadelphia, and on December 23 Porter joined him at the home of a church member, A. Armstrong and his family, who took a special liking to Porter's honest, open ways. As Porter left them he sensed he would see this family again. He then led Joseph's group back to Washington.

In early January 1840 the documents arrived. Joseph finally had his evidence: 491 testimonies by his people claimed a damage total of $1,381,044. Included was Porter's $2,000 for the three Missouri farms he'd been forced to leave, plus $3,000 for his parents' farms. Joseph and Porter then delivered the evidence to the congressional committee.

The congressional spokesman promised to report the results to Joseph at his boarding house that very day.

At their boarding room Joseph, Porter and the others awaited the results, but no one came as promised. Joseph and

Porter returned three days later to the Capitol Building and received their reply.

Simply, "No."

The committee had carefully considered the proposed claims, but flatly rejected the request.

Joseph and Porter left the Capitol without a word. Porter knew he himself could live without the funds, but on the walk to the boarding house he glanced several times at Joseph, who was feeling the kingdom financially crumbling out from under him. So many of the poorest Mormons had incurred terrible debts from their persecutions, and now their hopes of being repaid and therefore freed from the bondage of their obligations would be dashed. Porter felt the pressure Joseph was feeling, and outside their boarding house they stopped. Porter gave him a hug.

"It'll be all right, old friend."

Joseph forced a small smile, "You're right. It's never the end of the world, is it?" Suddenly Joseph gave him a huge bear hug and picked him up. "Of course it's not the end of the world!"

Porter laughed and began cheering. Joseph also broke into a cheer. When they arrived in their room they greeted several others — their party had grown to include Orson Pratt — and Joseph announced with great merriment, "They've turned us down!"

Porter shouted, "But all we could do is try, eh brethren?"

The others smiled politely, bewildered.

Orson Pratt caught their spirit. "Three cheers for the kingdom! Though Congress may fail us, the Lord never will!"

Joseph's enthusiasm was contagious: "We will yet win the battle. We will be a happy and prosperous people!"

All five shared his excitement and cheered in unison as Porter led them: "Hip, hip, hooray! Hip, hip, hooray! Hip, hip, hooray!"

Joseph bellowed, "May the journey back to our families begin!"

On their return home, the wintry, humid Eastern blasts went right through them. The men shivered inside the carriage while Porter all but froze driving it. His mind meanwhile felt scorched, riveted with hot nails to Luana and the children. Francis Higbee had remained in Washington to press the government a while longer — just in case some committeeman changed his mind — while Orson Pratt also stayed in the East, preparing to leave on a mission to Liverpool, England March 9, 1840, only weeks away. They sold the carriage in Pennsylvania and took a train to Dayton, Ohio.

There, the train came to a halt just after noon. Joseph's group debarked the steam-powered vehicle.

At the station, Porter gave most of his carriage money to Joseph. "Use it for the others to get home," he told Joseph. "Then if there's any left, give it to my wife."

Joseph admired Porter's generosity, but was surprised by his announcement.

"Where're you going?" inquired Foster.

Porter turned and faced his three companions: "My sister, Caroline, lives in Hamden, Ohio and I promised her a long time ago I'd stay a few days if I got here again. We were real close growing up."

Foster was angry. He and Rigdon had felt secure with Porter on the trip, despite Porter's quietly critical feelings towards them whenever they complained. "Can't you just visit your sister one or two days? We'll wait for you," said Foster.

Porter did not respond, but he was actually afraid of returning home and facing Luana. Nor did he wish to burden Joseph by informing him of Luana's complaints that Porter was his bodyguard.

He knew his hesitancy to return was based on more than having to face his wife with all their problems: He felt a nagging fear that . . . Luana might not be home when he returned.

He knew now, more than ever, that he actually did deep down love her.

And just how much, for the first time in his life, scared him.

CHAPTER 8

Porter made his way to Nauvoo, Illinois in early March 1840, several days after Joseph's arrival of March 4. Had he known Luana's thoughts — of him deserting his friends in Ohio and procrastinating his return to her — he would have pursued a different course.

When he did arrive he gazed at his cabin as it appeared around a neatly laid-out city corner. He stared at it as if it were a distant dream. He was relieved to see the yard somewhat cluttered with a lived-in look.

Through the window he spotted Luana. He remained out in the cold a minute, studying her. He breathed an audible sigh; nonetheless, he felt his heart beating furiously as he approached the front door.

He opened it and entered.

Luana was cleaning the brick oven. She turned and simply stared, then forced a cool smile. She walked to him and gave him a mechanical kiss.

He felt a faint nausea.

"Sit down," she offered.

They both sat.

"Where're the children?"

"At the neighbors — playing," she answered. "They'll be in presently for supper."

"Which neighbors — I'll get them."

She said nothing.

"Could we get them sooner than supper?" he said.

She ignored him.

He was curious.

"They've been quite well, Porter."

He fumbled for words, trying to think of what to say, given her unusual demeanor. Finally:

"What about the place here?" he said. "'It been all right?"

She studied him a minute. "Why didn't you return with Joseph and the others?"

"'Felt you'd be mad, and 'wasn't ready for it yet."

Luana did not blink an eye.

"Also," continued Porter, "I got to see my sister Caroline in Hamden. But my sister Emily was out of town."

"Is Caroline doing well?" said Luana coolly.

"Yeah, but she and her husband are sure against the church now. It made me sick. We was real close as kids." Luana noticed tears in his eyes.

"And I reckon," said Porter, "I'll prob'ly never see them again. This life or the next." Porter's belief was that families would only be together if sealed by church authorities, which power, like the church itself, had been restored to the earth by specific angels — the Biblical characters Elijah, Peter, James and John. "I got a feeling I'll never see her again anyway." He thought another moment and looked down. "They sure got beautiful little ones. I need to go see Mama and tell her about them; maybe she'll write more letters and can soften their hearts."

Luana squinted slightly and gazed off: She was disgusted that he did not have it in him to ask directly how she had been. She flushed away her feelings with a look of amusement.

He kept glancing at her, then searched for the baby. Orrin DeWitt Rockwell was now five months old. Porter saw him on the bed, picked him up, and hugged him. A tear trickled down his cheek. Except for Orrin DeWitt's first two days on the planet, Porter had missed the first five months of his boy's life.

As he gazed into his blue eyes, the boy's future seemed to flash before him. He felt a love for this baby he'd actually fought while being away from him, for fear of further pain. The longing for his two daughters suddenly stretched his soul. His thoughts of Emily, especially, anguished him. He could not bear to be away from her again.

"Where are the others?" he asked softly.

Luana told him, and he struck out for a neighbor's home. On his journey he found the city lots filling up and neatly arrayed; he observed the city mushrooming; he could see workers constructing homes even more elaborate than his parents'. When he found his daughters in a backyard, his heart pounded; they noticed him and ran to his arms.

He held them on his shoulders and twirled them. Emily squealed with delight as Porter felt the biggest lump in his throat he had ever felt.

He was home.

Almost immediately, he was perturbed at the amount of farmwork needing attention. In July 1840 Luana announced she was pregnant again. Impatient with people and life in general, because of her condition, she would direct her rages at Porter. He would find it convenient to visit Joseph even more often. He would usually pause near the Homestead and gaze downhill onto the Mississippi River before entering Joseph's home. He found his visits with Joseph increasingly interesting:

In August 1840 one John Cook Bennett was converted to the church. Joseph found in him a willing statesman. Porter could not figure the man out — and did not exactly trust him — but had no grounds to speak his suspicions to Joseph.

The prophet, by contrast, was delighted with Bennett, who lobbied to the Illinois state legislature and incorporated Nauvoo into a city. And from that nifty piece of paperwork was able to organize for Joseph his Nauvoo Legion, with Joseph appointed Lieutenant General, the highest ranking militia commander in the entire state (and technically in the entire nation among all the country's militias) which could prove fairly handy in case the state's armed forces were martialled for any reason, particularly against the saints. Because of Bennett's masterful stroke, Joseph's legion could acquire 500 firearms and three cannon from the state, which it soon did. For his industriousness, Bennett was elected the city's first mayor February 1, 1841. The Legion was officially organized three days later. Nauvoo was now larger than Chicago, and to the concern of neighboring non-Mormons, it was the state's largest city and a political entity with which to be seriously reckoned.

Porter was given free reign to attend Joseph's city council meetings but, while he usually did attend them, he had nothing to contribute. He always remained silent, not feeling enough confidence before others to speak his political mind, nor had he much of an interest in dull, daily civic matters. His heart was elsewhere. His thoughts usually drifted to life on the river.

He rarely performed domestic chores, yet wished to assist Luana. So, awakening this day in a particularly merry mood, he decided to make her breakfast. It was a miserable concoction of over-cooked eggs, burned bacon, and crumbly bread made worse by butter being beaten onto it with a large knife, such that it resembled an awkward-looking, churned up tortilla.

Luana cringed, but ate it.

Afterwards, he held the baby boy and, though it was his first son, he still felt somehow closer to Emily. For some reason he had not bonded in the same manner to Caroline either, perhaps because he had been absent most of her life compared to Emily. Also, there was something simply magical about Emily that caused him to dote on her, to get up with her in the middle of the night since birth to hold her and later to fetch her drinks of water before Luana could muster herself to action. Emily simply held Porter's heart in the palm of her hands, and everybody saw it.

"Our new baby will need plenty of blankets," said Luana. "And that costs money. Will you be spending the entire day every day working the harvest so we can have cash?"

Porter finished picking up her breakfast plates and now sat across from her.

"I'm leaving the fields early today," he said.

"Why?"

"Business."

She knew that meant Joseph business.

"Guarding him somewhere again?"

"Not exactly."

"What exactly?"

"I'm joining the Nauvoo Legion."

"After all we've talked about, what with your work, and now taking care of your mother's acreage, and ours, and bodyguarding Joseph on his little excursions into the country for heaven knows what, you're now joining the army?"

"That's what I said."

"How can you even think about such a thing?"

"Easy. It's what needs to be done."

"Can't you think about what I need done?"

"We've talked about that, and I thought you supported me."

"I agreed on a lot — even though we don't have half what we need — but now you're actually going off and joining the Legion? Can't we both have a say in this?"

"I've made up my mind."

"Your time is your family's, Porter; it seems we should help you decide what you do with your time, and especially when it effects how we live and everything about us."

"I think you're overstepping your bounds here."

"Overstepping what bounds? Have you set bounds on what I can and cannot be concerned with? How dare you take that attitude!"

"I just mean with what I do with my time," he said. "Am I a prisoner to you?"

"You're my husband — the children's father — so don't you feel any responsibility to take care of us?"

"How can you even think I don't take care of you? I don't see anyone starving around here. I don't see anyone not clothed!"

"Because I make do with what we have!" she said. "Sure, you get the food we need, but how many times do I have to hammer into you that we need more?"

"Maybe if you quit hammering, things would be different."

He went outside to his horse. She followed, slamming the door behind her.

"What do you mean by that?" said Luana. "If I quit 'hammering,' just how would things be different?"

He said nothing.

"Different in how I talk to you?" she said. "That's the only thing that *would* be different!"

"Maybe if you did, I'd want to spend more time here."

"You're claiming how I talk to you determines this thing with Joseph?"

"I don't know what you're talking about," he said.

"It's your loyalty to everything Joseph asks or wants that makes you this crazy."

"Then you're probably right," he said cinching his saddle to his horse.

"No, I want to know what you meant. You're saying it's how I talk to you that causes you to do what you do? You expect me to believe that?"

He whirled on her. "Only a fool could put up with your constant pecking and trying to lock me into a jail. How could any man on earth live with that? I'm getting out of here." Porter untied his horse.

"Papa, Papa!" yelled Emily, followed by curious little Caroline, who repeated her sister's same words like a parrot. They both ran to Porter's leg and grabbed it.

"I'll be back later this week, honies. You be good."

"Where're you going?" said Emily.

Luana cut her off, shouting, "Later this week? You're going to desert us for *days!*" How are we going to collect the crops till then?"

"They'll be all right."

"They're turning now — the first frost is overdue!"

"Don't worry about them — we've got enough food for the winter."

"Extra crops are the only thing I've got to barter for cash with, Porter! We need every extra root and vegetable we can muster!"

"Then I'll muster what's left when I get back."

"How dare you leave us this way!"

"I'll dare to do anything I darn well please, and while I'm at it, you can quit talking to me like this in front of the kids. *My* kids deserve seeing respect from their ma."

"Respect for what? You telling me off for how I barely make do, when you're deserting them?"

"Don't say I'm deserting them, Luana."

"Then what's so important about going on another assignment for Joseph?"

"This one's gotta be done right."

She looked at him curiously.

"Bandits are raiding farms of non-Mormons out in the county and blaming us for it. Joseph says we've got to cut 'em off — find them and get them to confess their crimes—before they bring whole mobs down on us. In case you haven't noticed, the newspapers are getting as mean as ever about us —but you can think I'm just going out there to waste my time all you want."

"Joseph's friends are leaving the church," said Luana, "and exposing what he's doing. That's all the newspapers are writing about."

"How can you talk that way?" shouted Porter. "Exposing what? Those men are dissenters to the truth and they're turncoats, taking lies to the newspapers, just like in Independence. How can you even think that way in my house, much less talk that way in front of my kids!"

"I've read the newspapers myself," said Luana. "Which is more than what you can say."

Porter's not being able to read was an issue upon which she had never touched.

"I know what I know. I don't need to read nothin'!" Angrily he led his horse out of sight, disappearing with it around the corner of the house to fill his canteen in the back yard well.

Emily and Caroline turned their looks to Luana, who watched Porter disappear around the house. Luana ran to catch up with him.

"I know you don't want to be gone from the children this long!" She strode towards Porter, who was already at the well, hauling up the water bucket one quick pull at a time.

"Then why do you think I'm doing it?" he said.

"I don't know."

"I need to help Joseph."

"It's deeper than that, isn't it?" she said.

"Nothing needs to be deeper."

"Your father? Is this about him?"

"It's only about doing the right thing," said Porter.

"And for you isn't the right thing revenge?"

He stopped pulling up the water bucket and gazed at her.

"Porter, you've got to let go of this. Our enemies are not the only ones to blame!"

"They drove my father out in the cold and that's why he's in the ground!"

"Porter, you're blaming all Missourians, but they didn't kill your father. Joseph says the war was going to happen no matter what we did. It was a matter of the Kingdom of God having rocks thrown at it."

He finished pulling up the water bucket and strode to his horse.

"Porter, if you go off to fight those bandits in the countryside, right when I need you here the most, when you return, the children and me will not be here."

"I've heard the warning before."

"So you don't think I'll go through with it?"

"You don't have the heart to take Emily away from what she loves most." Porter perceived he had cut into Luana deeply — he had often seen her envy of his relationship with Emily.

"I would take her away in a second," exclaimed Luana. "When she gets away from you she'll see for the first time in her life what she needs to see!"

"Mama," broke in Emily, "what are you talking about?"

Luana searched for Emily's voice appearing from behind the house.

"Don't worry, honey," said Luana. "Go in and watch little Orrin and Caroline."

"Papa?" said Emily. "Are we going to see you again?"

Porter's anger escalated as he mounted up and turned to face Luana. "You even think about taking her away . . . " He choked back the rest of his words.

"I'm doing more than thinking," said Luana. "I am warning you here and now, as clear as I can, that you have your choice. If you go off to fight Joseph's holy war against the bandits, when you return — if you return alive—I will be in Independence with my parents, and the kids will be with me for good!"

"You can't scare me with hollow threats," he said.

"What have I got to live for here?"

"You've got something to die for if you leave," he added.

"You're threatening me?"

"You can take it how you like," said Porter. "But my children are never again setting foot in Missouri!"

"We'll just have to see how far your craziness will go. And if you'll even hate your own children for becoming Missourians. 'Cause that's where I'm raising them the minute you leave us."

"You will be here when I get back," yelled Porter, "and you will have a hot meal prepared for me the hour I do. We are staying here no matter what! I say what we do on my property! And I say who our enemies are! You can either join me or fight me, but anybody who fights me will live to regret it, if they live at all!" Porter turned his horse and galloped away.

Emily stood staring at her father, unsure what to make of all this and expecting him to return any minute for her.

Luana's tears flowed as she watched the horse's hooves beating down the muddy road, disappearing around the bend. She knew, having drawn the battle lines, there was no turning back. The question was when. She ripped off the necklace Porter had given her as her wedding gift, and traipsed down to the river bank, then tossed it with all her strength out into the wide Mississippi.

CHAPTER 9

Standing atop his roof, Joseph faced the 2,000 strong Nauvoo Legion in his uniform, his sword held to the sky.

Porter arrived late and stood on the back row.

"Will you stand by me to face our enemies?" said Joseph to the crowd.

The legionnaires shouted as one, "Yes!"

"Then I challenge us one and all to treat our neighbors outside the city as friends, and to embrace with kindness even those who declare themselves to be our enemies. We must be not only soldiers of freedom, but of light. Will you accept that challenge?"

"Yes!" cried the crowd.

Porter, however, squinted at Joseph, feeling the strongest hatred ever for their enemies, a flame which seemed eternally lit by the memory of his father.

As the legion disbursed, some men made their way forward to visit Joseph, who had by now descended a ladder from the roof.

Porter spotted three men leaving, whispering curiously among themselves — Francis Higbee (who had accompanied him to Washington, D.C.), Wilson Law and William Law. Porter thought he heard something about a "trap being laid," and wandered briefly what kind of trap they were talking about, but he dismissed it, not making sense of it. He trusted them as Joseph's close associates. Still, he glanced back at them, wondering what they were up to. He then searched for his commander of the raid against the thieving bands. It was his old Jackson County neighbor David Pettegrew, who now assigned Porter as the leader of 12 legionnaires to patrol the road that night to Carthage.

"Why have me lead the band?" said Porter, fearing he might instigate an all-out war considering his feelings over his father.

"Joseph trusts you with this," said Pettegrew.

Porter appreciated the confidence and nodded:

"I won't let him down."

Two hours later he rode at the front of the dozen legionnaires, all out of uniform, wearing leather coats and brim hats, trotting briskly on horseback and holding rifles.

The purpose of their assingment was to put an end to the worse kind of thievery — that which blackened the name of their people and their city. Joseph had received a report from non-Mormon farmers in Hancock County that self-proclaimed "Mormon bandits" were attacking nearly every night — raiding farms and stealing animals. Sometimes, their faces covered with bandannas, they broke into homes and stole valuables.

Porter had figured out a pattern to their recent robbings, and decided to hide in a thicket beside the road leading to Carthage.

As they waited behind the tree grove, he assigned a lookout. They ate beef jerky in silence until just before full moon, when their guard rushed to them.

"It's time."

Porter was the first on his horse. He beheld eight strangers riding on the road ahead. Porter and the 12 silent legionnaires followed the strangers from a hundred yards back. After a mile they observed them pull up bandannas and turn off the main road toward a farmhouse.

Porter and his men followed. Being his first leadership assignment since Far West when he stole the militia's rifles, he determined to not let Joseph down. With a prearranged arm signal, half his riders split off to the left of the farmhouse, while Porter rode with his own group to the right.

The "bandanna raiders," as he called them, dismounted and rushed into the farmhouse. They stole coins and jewelry, threatened the non-Mormon family by telling them "in the name of Joseph, keep quiet!" then rushed outside to their horses.

Before they could mount up, they were met with a voice 20 yards away:

"Drop your weapons, boys!"

The bandits instead pulled up rifles and fired toward the voice. Their shots missed. Panicking, they ran to their right to the cover of a thicket.

From there, half of Porter's men stepped out and faced them with six rifles aimed.

The eight bandits stopped. Several turned to run to the left — but Porter and the other half of his force suddenly loomed in front of them.

The bandits, some facing to their left, others to the right, were confused. One took out running toward his horse. Porter lowered his rifle and fired, hitting the man's boot heel.

The impact of the lead ball knocked him head over heels in a somersault. The fellow stood, turned to face Porter, and held his rifle in the air with one hand.

"I hate repeating myself, boys," said Porter.

"Drop it!" yelled the bandits' leader to his own men.

All eight rifles dropped.

Porter strode to their leader. "Give me what you've got!"

"Who are you," said the bandit leader, "Robin Hood or something?" The other bandits chuckled.

"Yeah, I rob from the rich," said Porter, and give to the poor. Them." He nodded toward the farm couple emerging from their home.

"What did you folks have taken from you?" said Porter.

The husband, in his fifties and well-whiskered, stepped forward. "Who are you gentlemen?"

"Sent from Joseph Smith," said Porter.

"Wait a minute," said the farmer, looking at the bandits and focusing on their leader.

"I think," said Porter, "we oughta first see who we're talking to. Boys, pull down your bandannas."

The bandits were hesitant and stared at their leader.

"We're waiting," said Porter.

The leader lowered his bandanna, uncovering his face, and the others followed.

The farmer registered surprise. "Zeke Evans! And Tom Hanley McTeil! I've seen a couple of you others . . . I don't understand — you're Mormons?"

"You get word out to your neighbors," said Porter to the farmer, "that these boys have been representing themselves as us, but I think you see the difference." To the bandits he blurted, "Give them back what you stole."

He glanced at the one older bandit.

"You don't happen to be the Zeke that lived near Joseph Smith's farm in Palmyra, New York, are you?"

Zeke nodded sheepishly.

"Well ain't that interesting how the wheel turns," said Porter. "Last time we met, you were chasing me, only I barely came up to your elbow. Now, look who's got the drop on who?"

"I know you boys' fathers," interrupted the farmer. "I am awful ashamed for this. You've been terrifying the countryside but good, and everybody thinks it's these fellows," he added, nodding toward Porter's men. "Shame on you!" yelled the farmer. "Get off my property!"

On their ride home Porter felt proud he had been successful — a far cry from botching his attempt at sneaking in the shovel handle to Joseph, despite the eventual rescue from the sheriff. He knew, however, that the boys, led by his old nemesis, "Zeke," had raided too many farms across the county in recent weeks to halt completely the rumors that "Joseph's boys" were to blame. It would take a major event to turn the tide.

"I don't know about you," said Porter to his men as they rode home at a brisk trot under the moonlight, "but I think those boys will likely strike again — or others like 'em — and they'll keep using us for cover. Nathan," he said to his neighbor, "you take over tomorrow — and every Tuesday — and you boys," he said pointing to each of the next several. "Will you lead our group out on the other nights?" He then assigned specific days to each. "I'll take Mondays when I'm in town; otherwise, Nathan, will you cover me?" His neighbor nodded with determination. Porter continued, "We'll patrol every road in the county if we have to. And if we can't protect our neighbors good enough, I'll get Joseph to send out another band like ours every night — and more if necessary — to protect the innocent folk and stop the bandits from blaming us."

Porter returned to his cabin, relieved to find Luana home asleep with the children. He wondered if and when she actually would leave . . .

She opened her eyes as he prepared for bed. "Don't think I'm backing down on my threat to leave. I happened to have found out tonight I'm probably having another child. But that will only delay the inevitable."

"Another child?" he smiled. Then said, "Where's your necklace?" He noticed immediately it was gone from her neck. She had only taken it off to bathe ever since they'd been married.

"Gone forever," is all she said.

Porter felt simultaneously sick over her plans to leave him and elated over the news of another baby. He smiled once more, attempting, like his pa, to look for the best in any situation, especially given the possibility that she would change her mind *because* of the baby.

CHAPTER 10

The first sign of spring 1841 revealed itself as Porter aided in the delivery of another child: True to the custom, he brought water from the creek beside the house and boiled it. He noticed a warmth and concern within the neighbors' hearts that touched him. Several neighbors were willing to help any way they could.

Luana gave birth to Sarah Jane Rockwell March 25, 1841. (Author's note: Heretofore, a common error among historians has been to date her birth as 1842.) As before, he sat outside his cabin while his mother and a younger sister attended Luana. And again, Emily sat with him, replacing his father. Little Sarah delighted him, and had a personality different of course from those of his other children, but Emily still held his heart the most, and she hung on him like a flea to a dog.

Porter enjoyed the simplicity of life around his children and was becoming more settled than he had ever thought. The monotony of farm work was broken with weekly Legion drills.

He found them exhilarating. He learned from Joseph that no more bandits had been found and their activities had apparently ceased due in part to Porter's efforts, but the damage had been done: Most of the old locals still blamed Joseph's people for the thieving raids.

As the weeks passed, Porter looked forward even more to Friday drills. But his hours of call for bodyguard duties became minimal as Joseph increasingly recruited armed legionnaires to take the burden off Porter and his family. Joseph wanted Porter home at nights with Luana.

By the summer of 1841, over 8,000 saints lived in the area.

Luana complained of Ugly eating more food than they could afford — even though the dog still lived primarily off wild creatures; however, its favorite terrain — the glorious swamp — had been drained over the months, becoming practically non-existent in Nauvoo, causing him to travel miles away. He was now no spring puppy, so the task of feeding off wild swamp life was becoming a formidable one; thus, he was resurrecting his old art form of begging. He essentially sucked it up and settled for the goodies of questionable quality at the Rockwell residence. Luana always gave in and fed him left-overs, but those left-overs were the stuff from which she made her nightly stew; so, Ugly was literally eating them out of house and home.

"That dog stays," said Porter.

"Then you'll starve the children," said Luana, "because Ugly is eating their food and all of them can't survive off it."

Porter knew there was no alternative. It was useless trying to get his wife to stretch their silver further — she had different spending habits than his and could not seem to make things work like his own mother.

"All right," said Porter, "I'll take him down the road to Mama's."

"No!" shouted Emily.

"You can still visit him, honey," said Luana, "all you want. He's still your dog."

"He's Pa's dog. Kicking him out is just like kicking out Pa."

Porter glanced at Luana, who held back a smile, then she proceeded to clean up the kitchen.

Porter called Ugly, and together they hiked down the road to his mother's, knowing she would take good care of the animal. The kids gathered at the porch and waved goodbye.

"You'll see him almost as much," said Porter, turning toward the porch. But he knew — as did they — that it would not be the same. They were used to falling asleep each night beside — and awakening each morning to — the large gentle creature's kindly manner and soft, thick fur. Porter was suddenly angry at not only Luana's money mismanagement but his own inability to make sufficient income to keep the animal for his children. Taking the dog away from them, as he watched their faces, was more discomforting than he had predicted.

"Come on, Ugly. Let's go faster."

"He's not as fast as he used to be," said Porter to his mother, now in her living room. "So he's not as good a hunter. That means he needs table scraps."

"We have plenty of food for him," said Sarah, kneeling and hugging the animal. "And I'll see to it Emily and the rest get to play with him often."

"I'll still be around for you, boy," said Porter. He left the dog on his mother's porch. As he departed, Ugly stared after him and whined. Porter turned. "Now you stay put. This is your new home."

Ugly seemed to understand.

"But you're still mine," Porter continued. "And I'll see you as much as I can. I love you, Ugly." Porter ambled away, upset over what had brought them to this condition. He kicked a rock beside the gravel road.

One afternoon while Porter was plowing east of town, he spotted Lyman Wight galloping across the field towards him. He could not understand what the blonde, sinewy soul was saying until Wight stopped his steed directly in front of him.

"They've kidnapped Joseph!"

Porter ran to his horse. He mounted bareback and galloped off beside Wight.

Emma Smith was in tears. She explained to the men that two Missouri deputies had absconded with Joseph, and he was being taken to Springfield, Illinois where the State Supreme Court would determine his outcome.

Porter and Wight galloped towards Hamilton, Illinois. On the road, they found Joseph and the two deputies. They also discovered two others of Joseph's friends who had caught up to them.

Joseph's eyes lit up when he saw his old friend: Porter rode beside him and glared at the Missourians. The deputies glanced away.

Porter issued a subtle threat towards the deputies: He played with a firearm, acting like he was cleaning it.

Joseph asked Porter to put it away, and explained he was safe.

"I'll be home in a few days," said Joseph. "They won't hold an innocent man like Missouri did."

He gave Porter a wink of assurance.

With Wight, Porter left the five men but followed for several hours out of sight and hearing range to the side, concealed by thick brush and trees. Finally, Porter recognized Joseph's wisdom. Illinois authorities seemed different than the Missourians. Porter glanced at his companion Wight, who accepted his silent command: They turned their horses back to Nauvoo.

It was spring 1842. Joseph's case was brought before Judge Steven A. Douglas and the case was dismissed. Joseph was released.

When he arrived at Nauvoo, Porter and others held a party. But Luana would not attend. She had over the past couple years — since moving to Nauvoo — slipped in her church attendance. It had in fact been several weeks since she had even graced a meeting with her presence, and she had begun criticizing church authorities, including Joseph, on both ecclesiastical and civic policies. She still overall believed the doctrines, but allowed her increasingly negative outlook — which she was the first to admit was the easiest way to withdraw from life and friends — to cloud her perspective.

Porter returned from the party late to find Luana still dressed and seated at the cabin table, feeding little Sarah.

She's big enough to travel, Porter. But I've watched you with her, and it honestly has softened me to see you with this child. So I've decided to give you one more chance. If you leave on any more of your wild assignments, I'm leaving on one of my own. Is that clear?"

He had forced himself to live with her daily criticisms for the children's sake, and tried whenever possible to avoid confronting her, just to keep peace in the family.

"Yes, dear," he said. "I am trying to cut down on the number of assignments for Joseph, and as you know, he's asked for my help less and less. Now, where's dinner?"

"No food, no dinner."

"What're you talking about?"

"Simple. We ran out of money — so we don't eat — except for our produce."

He felt himself getting angry. "I want bread and buttermilk. Not more produce."

"Then bring home money," she said.

"If I did, there would not be any left for bread and buttermilk next week."

"What do you mean by that?"

Despite his desire to keep peace, he broiled whenever he found her misusing money, and especially when she blamed him for their financial problems. So he could not resist holding back:

"Whatever silver I do bring home will be spent in a few days on stuff we don't need."

"How can you say we don't need what I buy?"

"My mama made do with lots of things."

"My folks had a higher standard of living, I'll admit that," she said. "But they knew good things to get."

"Well, Mama had a lot more kids and less help from Papa than your mama had, but she'd get by on whatever amount of silver we have."

"Hooray for your mama," she said.

"I'm just saying . . . "

"I know what you're saying. It's pretty obvious," she cut in. "You think I'm irresponsible."

"It just seems like the only way to make you happy is for you to spend all our money — and half of it on stuff we don't need."

"If you made more, we wouldn't have this problem."

"If I doubled our money you'd still spend it."

She sat down tearfully, deeply anguished.

Porter wondered if he'd gone too far.

"Are you all right?" he said.

She stared off.

"What's the matter?"

She blew out a long sigh and decided to say the inevitable, which came out softly:

"I can't live here anymore."

Porter paused a moment, collecting his thoughts:

"We could live at Mama's," he said. "Since Pa passed away she's got plenty of room, even with my brothers and sisters there."

"No thanks. Not in a million years. I have somewhere else to go."

Porter flushed.

"My father is getting older and may not be around much longer. I also want my mother to help raise the children. Two babies are too much for me and you're not willing to help."

Porter blew out a silent sigh and realized it would do no good to address that subject; they had argued over it before: How could he do domestic chores while working to bring in food and performing city and church duties? There was no time. There was no answer.

Time spent by him helping around the cabin was the most important time he could spend, she had maintained; so his priorities were lop-sided.

But how could he do other things that he is better suited for and still do all she wants, he would argue.

And so it went in circles. This time he said nothing to further the argument; he changed it:

"Luana, there's no church in Independence. We can't attend meetings there."

"I wasn't referring to both of us going."

Porter stared at her, stunned. "You said you wanted me to raise Sarah — and I have been cutting back on trips with Joseph, so do you think this idea of yours is fair?"

"It's fair for me to keep my sanity — and I can't keep it with our money problems." He felt a knot tighten in his stomach.

"So you're leaving over that?"

She glanced at him, then down. "You always were a little slow with the obvious."

He was in shock. "Who can we see to talk sense to you?"

"Talk sense to me? As if my decisions are crazy? It's settled — I'm leaving," she said. "If you come, that's your choice. But there's no work in Independence."

"You can't be serious — that's the heart of our worst enemies." Porter grabbed her arm. "We've talked about this before."

"And we've gotten nowhere," she said. "We hate each others' ideas and I'm wondering if it's even deeper."

"I'm heading to a week-long shooting contest down in St. Louey tomorrow. I'll win a month's supply of cash for five days work. When I get back, I'll give you all the cash, and we'll patch things up." He let go of her and left angrily, the cold wind whistling over him.

As Porter returned to his cabin eight days later at three AM he was certain she would be waiting for him. After all, he figured, it's more money she wanted, and that was the answer. Indeed, he had won the entire shooting match over several thousand frontier participants who had swarmed St. Louis for the event, and now he was happy to report back to her.

At home, he found his wagon and other two horses missing. He jumped from his horse and ran into the house. No Luana. No children.

No one. The fire was dead in the fireplace. He went to the door and gazed across the neighborhood. He realized Luana was by now already in Missouri and well on her way toward Independence. He blew out a silent sigh, then, with the bottom of his fist, pounded the door frame. He would just have to track them down.

CHAPTER 11

Porter rode in the moonlight toward Independence. March night winds cut like steel, but he was well bundled. With Independence a week away, he hoped to overtake Luana's wagon on the main road, yet soon realized the futility: She likely took a different route in order to not be discovered by him; furthermore, where she could travel without problems of being stopped, he had to be more discreet, pulling his horse off the road into the woods whenever strangers approached in order to not be recognized. Hundreds of old Missourians had known him as the barge boy at Big Blue, so he could not take any chances they or others he later fought might recognize him; thus he again faced the same concerns as his last trip into Missouri.

The going was slow and he slept little. He would ride each day till midnight — half the time in the woods near the road and the other half on the road itself. Even well off the road he'd camp with no fire, and eat only jerky and spring water.

A week later, two days shy of Independence, he espied two strangers approaching in the moonlight. He turned into thick woods and passed parallel to them. Because sound carries with greater amplification in the still night air, he could decipher their words:

"What'll we do with Smith once we get him?"

"All I care about is the bounty; they can do anything they want."

"'You sure we ain't wasting our time? Seems like sheriffs could just go across the river and nab him."

"But Illinois ain't cooperating with Missouri warrants, so only bounty hunters will be after him. I just hope we nab him before any other boys get to him."

Porter, secluded by the trees, watched the men riding past, going east toward Illinois. The men had referred to "other" bounty hunters, so he knew if he "sidetracked" these two there would still be an endless parade of other bounty hunters. Certainly Joseph had friends in Nauvoo who were looking out for him, although perhaps not on a regular basis. In any case, Joseph's wife Emma would always answer the door, or if neighbors were over — which they almost always were — they would. Suspicious characters such as these, Porter figured, would never make it to Joseph's presence. At least not theoretically. Additionally, Joseph had a secret room set aside for such events. But if Porter himself were there to protect him, the chances of bounty hunters succeeding were zero. His blood broiled, torn over whether to return to Nauvoo and warn Joseph or to keep going west to Independence. He gazed down the dirt road toward Independence, where he knew his family was arriving. He looked eastward again toward Nauvoo . . . toward Joseph . . . and then began riding . . . toward Independence.

Around a familiar bend he arrived. There, he recalled his first encounter with Luana years earlier amidst splotches of spring snow in the trees, just as he was seeing tonight. He presently arrived at Luana's parents' farm. As he hitched his horse to a post, Emily and Caroline ran outside.

"Papa!" shouted Emily.

He knelt. Both girls ran to him and hugged him. As he kissed them, Luana watched from the doorway. She felt a twinge in her chest but fought it.

At the cabin door he arrived to little Orrin and lifted him. Orrin's eyes lit up and Porter hugged him. Then he spotted baby Sarah, who squeaked. Porter squeezed her, then lifted her into the air.

Luana looked down and away.

CHAPTER 12

At the dinner table Porter sat in silence. Luana's parents were posted at the opposite end, his girls and little Orrin DeWitt sat to his left, while Luana sat with baby Sarah Jane to his right. They ate catfish and cornbread.

"Awful good grub," he offered.

"Thank you," blurted Olive Beebe curtly. Porter was in her mind an uninvited guest, having arrived an hour earlier to obviously drag his wife back home against her will. Luana had insisted to her, however, that they be civil to her children's father.

Luana proceeded to speak to her parents as if Porter were not present, and in her voice was a distinct whine as she related her life in Nauvoo.

Porter resented it but said nothing. He suspected they had recently spoken negatively of him. He did not particularly like things said behind his back — and had no solid evidence of it — but it lingered in the air. He noted that his oldest two girls were reticent. With their large eyes they gazed upon these overly friendly strangers — her grandparents whom they had not seen in years — with shyness and wonder. Then Emily locked eyes on her father, and took over the dinner conversation, explaining how much she missed him.

Luana watched her oldest daughter laud over Porter.

"Finer catfish I've never found," said Porter after a pause, embarrassed over Emily's accolades. "It's Luana's finest dish."

"After my bread pudding," said Luana.

"Right, after your bread pudding," said Porter.

Luana's father, Isaac, was short with his answer:

"Yeah, good catfish."

"Well," said Porter with a dry voice after regarding their coolness a moment, "things haven't changed much."

Nothing else was said among the adults. Emily and Caroline gave Porter an account of their day in detail and he listened attentively.

After supper, as he braved the bread pudding, he excused himself and went outside to the outhouse. On the way, he heard Luana and her mother at the well on the other side of the property. They did not know he was in hearing range.

"All right," said Olive, "he can stay, but only in the barn a few days."

It was night. As Luana showed Porter his quarters beside the cow, she carried a torch.

"Right over there it's dry," she said. "You're welcome to some blankets."

"'Brought my own," he mumbled, pulling them off his horse onto the straw.

"Well," she sighed, "My folks are hospitable but only to a point. I hope you don't over-stay your welcome."

"As soon as you and the kids come back with me, we'll be out of their hair," he muttered.

"You know where I stand on that."

"I think you're forgetting about the kids," he said, louder.

"I have been thinking of the kids as a matter of fact, but my sanity is just as important."

"Our kids are most important," said he.

"I need a safe place."

"Your place is with me."

"My place is where I can live and not be miserable."

"Your people — our people — are home, Luana."

"This is home now."

"With your husband is home."

"That's your opinion, but I'm staying here."

"You made your choice with me a long time ago," he said.

"And I make a new choice now. Whether you stay is your choice."

Porter gaped at her with eyes wide: He could not believe this was happening.

"Why would you stay here?" he said incredulously.

"That's where all my memories are — that's all I have now."

"And your memories with me?"

"I'd rather not talk about them."

"What about Nauvoo?"

"I think the answer is obvious."

"You don't want to return even later?" He then looked straight at her and implored her with his eyes.

She turned away, "Maybe in the next life — certainly not this one." She smiled, then began walking towards home.

He stared at the open door a moment, went to it and called out, "What about us moving just out of Nauvoo and making new memories?"

She turned to face him and walked slowly backwards toward her house, "I've had all the memories I can handle. Sorry."

Porter stood staring at the very door he had knocked upon ten and a half years previously, the door of hope, excitement, and feelings upon which he had pondered. "He finally spoke up. "Even though the Spirit of the Lord bore witness to you on the truth of Joseph's work," said Porter, "you've found a new home?"

She had no response, but tears welled up. She finally said, "I hope *you* find work, because the kids won't see you if you have to move back to Nauvoo."

He spoke louder, "You think on what I said. Those three girls and little Orrin need me as their pa."

"I've thought on that longer than you'll ever imagine. Understand this will likely be the last time Emily and the others may ever see you, so make the evening visits good. Good night." She turned with the torch and walked toward the cabin, leaving him in darkness.

When he watched her return to her parents' house, he could not decipher the comment she made to her mother, but when they both laughed, he broiled.

Falling asleep that night, Porter thought about Luana's and her mother's laughter until it ate into him like acid. In the middle of the evening he awakened in a cold sweat.

The next morning Luana returned to the barn with a bucket of water:

"This is to bathe with," she said. "You can use the well for drinking water."

"Or we can both drink in Illinois where there's better-tasting water," said Porter.

"I'm comfortable with the water here," she retorted.

"I want you and the children where everything in life is better."

"That's here."

"The children deserve the best home," said Porter.

"I agree with that — and that's here, too."

He was incensed, but spoke in a whisper so her parents could not hear: "Luana, pack up and make the move where you belong."

She lashed out with a bitter retort, "I'll be dead first," then retreated to her house. Out the doorway he caught sight of her parents watching and listening from their door. Her mother attempted holding back a resentful glare.

Porter glanced at Isaac Beebe, and the older man remained expressionless. A closer inspection of his face reflected in the dawn's light revealed a deep anger.

Porter knew he was up against almost impossible odds. All he could think of was to pray. And he relized that was something new for a man used to taking things into his own hands.

CHAPTER 13

Porter searched for work all day — no one would hire him. He returned to Luana's parents' farm to visit his children at dark. He was cold and hungry. Luana invited him inside for supper, but the conversation went quickly cold. Afterwards, he presented Luana all the money he'd earned from the St. Louis shooting contest, suggesting she spend it on cloth for the children's clothes and for staples. Luana thanked him for the coins and assumed a slight smile, but she would not look at him directly. She saw the cash as a feeble peace offering, and wondered where it was during their marriage.

Porter left to sleep in the barn, thinking deeply. He missed his mother and siblings. He also missed the society of his people, including Joseph. He felt like a slave here, dependent on the "kindness" of his in-laws. He not only felt complete disrespect among them but was practically here against his will. And it was draining him.

He recalled the previous night's conversation with his wife. Perhaps Luana had a point. As he remembered the countless hours he'd spent away from her, he could see the slow, down-hill retreat of her heart from his, although ironically the years had tendered his heart more towards her.

He realized he had only one solution, despite her opposition — he had to immediately leave the state with his family. It was obvious to him that, short of forcing her, she would not leave unless she changed her outlook on their relationship. He therefore decided to embark on a whole new strategy: He would treat her with the utmost kindness and charm.

That evening he felt a slight hope that he could make things right. Luana smiled appreciably as he related several amusing incidents in Nauvoo. He then recalled their early courtship and the hours he'd spent trekking the long road after work each day to see her. Her eyes revealed a faint glimmer of light.

Down a country lane he walked the next morning, fearing he could get no employment and therefore would have to leave the state too soon, before he could even receive divine intervention to melt her heart. He felt a sickening lump in the pit of his stomach. Roosters crowed and he was hungry. He recalled yesterday's failed attempts to gain employment, and knew it would be almost impossible today as well. The state's tight money policy, incorporated by the recently replaced Governor Boggs, was causing the economy to reel, and many citizens were struggling to feed their families because of the poor employment picture. Porter heard gripes and mumbles from several merchants, using the economy as an excuse to not hire him.

As the sky lightened and the sun burst through thin, darkened winter tree limbs, he strode down the hard, frozen road to a dilapidated farm a mile away.

"Got work?" said Porter to a 50 year old farmer, tall, lank and grey.

"Sorry," said the farmer, shaking his head.

Fifteen miles up more dirt roads, north and east, Porter came to a man of 70.

"What can I do to help?" said Porter.

"'Nothing to do."

"I see a hundred things."

"I see two hundred," said the man. "But 'got no money or food to pay you."

Porter blew out a sigh. "That's the tenth time I've heard this since dawn."

"The next fellah up the road, he'll be the eleventh."

Porter decided to help the old fellow for free the rest of the day, carrying heavy items and performing arduous tasks that the fellow was no longer able to do. Porter didn't even expect a thanks but, at the end of the day, did receive one. He nodded in return and strode onward.

With a hat shading most of his face and his head bent low, a thought crossed his mind about the old ferry, and then about his former cabin. Though he had earlier told himself he would not bother to visit the old homestead, he knew deep down he must.

Moving along the road to the structure he wondered if it still stood and who dwelled there, if anyone. The feeling he had as he walked through the grey wintry countryside — although it was technically spring — was almost ethereal: The trees were dark and still, the wind had stopped, and the sharp coldness lingered. He was left in a silence that allowed him to hear his own footsteps on the frozen, muddy road.

Around the last bend he walked, and suddenly came upon his old farm. The cabin was just as he'd left it: a deserted, burned shell. The door was still open. He ambled in. Feeling with his hands the walls he had constructed himself, he was surprised at how small the house was. He realized each home he had built — except for the small cabin at Quincy — had been larger, the construction more sophisticated, and the structural elements increasingly solid.

He then fought through the brush a hundred yards and came to his first Missouri residence — his parents home. It, too, was deserted and partially burned. He entered and gazed around. He recalled the excitement he had felt upon its completion, and now reflected on it's construction with his father; he wondered if his own children could ever look with that same fondness on him. He doubted it, and felt guilt at his absences from them. He loved his father and missed him, and now looked forward to returning to his mother. He had during this Missouri period visited his parents often, far more than he had after they had moved to Illinois. He loved the years here with his parents. Through the house he could hear an echo of his mother speaking of the neighbors and of news of their friends — and he missed it all. Such small things in life he had taken for granted but they now seemed priceless. He suddenly realized he was filling himself with sentiment. He left the cabin quickly. As he re-entered the woods, he glanced back one last time. The cabin, indeed the entire farm, was covered with weeds. It was the last established holding of his life before the turn of events that had swept him into marriage and now full circle back to Independence. He fought his tears.

As he walked through thick brush to the road leading to the river, his heart pounded. The old ferry dock was just ahead. He soon smelled the river, and finally spotted a clearing, then . . . there it was . . . the Big Blue River. He was almost afraid to look at it, but his eyes went straight for the ferry landing.

The dock was clean and well-kept, and the old hut where he'd thought for countless hours and visited with neighbors David Patten and David Pettegrew many a lazy afternoon was also in good shape. A man was seated at a campfire beside it. As he approached him he was surprised to see a barge across the river.

"Need service, sir?" said the fellow, politely standing.

"No thank you," said Porter.

"You're just seeing if we was in working order in case you needed us then?"

"Something like that."

"You live hereabouts?"

"Abouts."

The man perceived he was not getting a great deal from him and sat back at his fire. "Well, have a good day then."

"The ferry site," said Porter.

The man looked up. "What about it?"

"How did you come by it?"

"Well it sort of fell into my hands," he chuckled. "The Mormons left 'few years back and my uncle paid for it at auction. Got it for five dollars. Not much use for it anymore, not since they all left — but it keeps flour money for me and the wife. Prices are always going up, you know; that fool Boggs done us in pretty good with his tight money policy, but we keep a farm on the side and —"

Porter interrupted, "Who's ferry is it now?"

"What do you mean, who's ferry? I told you — it's my ferry."

"Where did it come from?"

"I told you."

"I mean the boat itself?"

"Oh, that was part of it — another reason it was so doggone cheap — it was sunk when I took it over — and damaged pretty good — but I salvaged it all right."

Porter merely stared at him, then began backing away. The fellow stood again and gazed after him.

Porter came to a stop. "'Plan to sell it?"

"Never."

He gazed over the ferry one last time, then glanced at the road in front of him and resumed walking.

He would not have attempted re-procuring it even if he could. Too many painful memories. And good memories best forgotten. His enemies, of course, would recognize him if he did resurrect life on the river.

The ferryman seemed baffled and watched him walk away and disappear.

CHAPTER 14

Not far from the Beebe residence — a mile west of their farm — Porter heard a man yelling. As he approached the stable he noticed the fellow struggling with a horse and swearing. Porter strolled up and greeted him. The horse bucked harder.

"Excuse me, sir," said Porter.

"I'm busy, if you can't see it," said the fellow, distraught and sweating.

"Beautiful horse," said Porter.

"He's a devil."

"Then maybe I got something in common with him. At least my wife would say so."

Cyrus Ward smiled, caught off-guard. He was kindly-looking and a bit porky with long ashen sideburns. "Well, I give up on him. He won't get broke."

Porter climbed the corral fence and ambled towards the animal, not looking at it directly but from the corner of his eyes as he approached it using his peripheral vision and going sideways.

"What're you doing?" said Ward.

"Wild animals don't like to be walked right up to or even looked right at. Not even me," he smiled. He got right up to the animal and stroked it.

"That's really something," said Ward. "I figured we was all in a big pecking order, and had to show the animals who was boss."

"Good way to view things," said Porter, "if you don't want to get anywhere with them."

"Can you do more with this animal?" said Ward.

Porter grabbed the lariat Ward had dropped into the mud, then placed it over the horse's neck. The horse grunted and slightly bucked.

"Whoa . . . " said Porter softly. "Come over here, boy. That's it."

"You work magic," said Ward. "What's your name?"

Given his danger, Porter suddenly realized he had not figured how to answer that question. He paused a moment. "Brown."

"That's all?"

"Yep."

"Mine's Ward."

"Glad to know you."

Cyrus Ward gazed curiously at him. Porter realized he had been stupid to not even disguise himself. All it would take is one person to recognize him.

"I've never seen any man deal with that animal," said Ward. "Are you looking for work?"

"Yes, sir."

"All right. You break in that horse — plus a few others I've got — and I'll feed you two meals a day and give you lodging."

"You've got a deal, mister," said Porter.

As he walked to the Beebe home at dusk, Porter realized just how precarious his situation was. He had managed to stay away from the general store he had frequented years earlier — although he did rather miss the kindly middle-aged proprietor — but he could not take chances. He resigned himself to tend Ward's stallion by day, visit his family at night, and to sleep back at Ward's till dawn, and all the while hope Luana would change her mind about returning to Nauvoo.

The concern he felt consuming him was Luana's heart knitting itself to the parents' old hearth; he noticed her every evening at dinner laughing with her mother. She was settling in very comfortably with old friends and ways. And Porter was forced to spend less and less time with her and the kids.

It was obvious of course she preferred her parents' company to his, and possibly always would. So he would have to step up his intensity, he thought, and perhaps make some bold move to get her attention.

In the center of Independence stood the stately home of ex-governor Lilburn W. Boggs. Inside the first floor, seated in his library and reading, Boggs turned the page to a good book which held his attention, his feet warmed by the crackling fire. Life did not get much better, he mused. But it did get better when his granddaughter brought him slippers and a cup of coffee laced with brandy. Suddenly a gunbarrel appeared at the window. It was slowly aimed at the back of his head . . .

When it blasted a lead ball straight toward his skull, Boggs jerked forward and over. His granddaughter screamed.

A shadow from the window disappeared. The moon cast the assassin's shadow as it moved through lawns of nearby newly-built manors and around a corner. The shadow disappeared in thick woods a quarter mile away.

CHAPTER 15

"**P**orter," said Luana, approaching him in the barn just after sundown, "there'll be no dinner tonight."

"Where're the kids?" he said.

"Inside. We have to talk."

"You've come to your senses about going back with me?" said Porter.

"I want to know one thing," said Luana. "How could you do that to Lilburn Boggs?"

"Do what?"

"Despite what he did to our people?"

"What're you talking about?"

"Why would you shoot him?"

"Boggs was shot?" said Porter.

"You don't know about it?"

"How could I?"

"You've been gone since dawn, and you've been a little crazy since your pa died. I thought maybe you took it — "

He cut in, "I've got better things to do. I've been turned down on job after job till Cyrus Ward hired me for his horses. You want to check that out?"

"I believe it if you say you didn't pull the trigger."

"Boggs had hundreds of enemies," said Porter. "Look how his tight money policy hit farmers and contractors. He also had political and business enemies. Not just us."

"But you do admit you're an enemy?"

"He's too pathetic to be an enemy."

She studied him and finally nodded. "That's what I needed to hear. You've got to saddle up and get out of here."

"Why should I if you believe me?"

"Just do what I say!" she shouted.

"You think I'd leave you and the kids when I've got a job, and — "

"You don't understand," she said. "Ma and Pa can't handle your being — "

"*You* don't understand," he interrupted. "I have a new job, and if your folks can't handle me here, I'll just move. Ward said he'd like me to stay — and even bring the family — but the job is only a few days. I want you and the children to go with me back to Nauvoo next week. Visit all you want with your folks, but it's time to cut the apron strings, and — "

"Don't you think I've wanted to?"

"What's holding you back?" he said.

"You!"

"Me?"

"Deserting me!" she said.

"How can you mean that? When?"

"Again and again," she said. "You deserted all of us!"

"I am promising you things will be good again, and — "

"You're still blind to it, aren't you?"

"To what?"

"That's why I can't go back! You don't even see how you've done it!"

"How can you claim that?"

"You're as far off the face of the earth as any man could ever be."

"What do you mean?"

"To even look at you makes me ill. I never want to see you — ever."

He was shocked.

Seeing him wounded caused her tender feelings to surface for him, but she fought them.

He felt sick from her attacks.

"Get out immediately," she said.

He had no words to respond.

She gulped, "Porter, a posse is coming for you."

Porter stared at her, aghast.

"I was not supposed to tell you. It was my parents' idea to get you captured by the sheriff after they heard the Boggs news."

"So why're you telling me all this if you don't care about me?"

"For the children's sake."

"You really care that little for me?"

"The feelings are gone. And I don't even want them back."

"Doesn't a commitment mean anything to you?"

"A ceremony?" she smirked.

"A covenant. We promised support for better or worse."

"Worse doesn't describe what I've got, and you're wasting your time. Get saddled and get out of here."

"Our people, our children, what are you giving up?" he said.

"I've got my children."

"Our children," he said. "They need us!"

"The posse will be here any minute!"

"You think it's for only the children's sake you're warning me?"

She glanced at him and said nothing.

"All right," he said. "If you won't come, I'm taking the children."

"With a posse on your trail? You're out of your mind!"

Luana's father, Isaac Beebe, suddenly appeared, stepping into the light:

"Who do you think you are, Luana, spoiling our plans?" Isaac raised a pitchfork and held it at Porter. "You stay put, Porter."

The pacifistic father of Luana, who had for so many years been her point of reference when arguing with Porter about mollifying his aggressions, was now steaming, eyes red.

Porter deflected the pitchfork and ran, then spotted Emily at the barn's doorway. He grabbed her and placed her atop his still-saddled horse. He whirled himself atop the roan and turned to ride out the wide door.

Luana screamed.

Just as they crossed the door's threshold, Luana's father reached behind Porter's back and grabbed Emily, then pulled her off.

Porter glanced down and saw Emily kicking and screaming. The older man walked backwards, away from the door. Porter then spotted on the road 80 yards distant the posse coming. He turned his horse towards the door. Still horseback, he grabbed Emily while simultaneously pushing over Isaac.

Emily reached towards Porter, but Isaac again jerked her away. Porter's hands were only a foot from her's.

Luana yelled, "Emily's in danger! Get out, now!"

"No!" shouted Emily. "Don't leave me!"

"She could be killed if you take her, Porter!" screamed Luana.

Porter glanced quickly from Luana to the posse closing in, then back at Emily, and realized for the first time in years that Luana just might be right.

"Honey," you think about me," said Porter to Emily, "and I'll be back for you. Just like I said at the campfire years ago. I told you I'd be back, and I was." He saw her crying and he turned away.

The posse was dead ahead, now 30 yards up the road and closing.

CHAPTER 16

Porter glanced at Emily one last time, then fixed his eyes on the posse and charged out in a gallop.

"Pa," yelled Emily. "Please take me!"

Porter heard her plaintive words but fought the voice stabbing him, and he tore right past the surprised posse.

Luana's mother Olive, still riding with the lawmen, was shocked when Porter dashed directly past her. He called back to her:

"Thanks, Mrs. Beebe. I've enjoyed your kindness, as always!"

The posse of six quickly stopped and turned their horses, then galloped off to catch him.

In the heart of Independence, not more than a half mile from the Boggs' residence, 500 men and women crowded a minister's front yard as he stood on his porch and faced the group:

"It is truth! Joe Smith hired Porter Rockwell to shoot Governor Boggs!"

The crowd booed the Mormons angrily.

"But," continued the minister, waving his large hands downward to quieten them, " . . . Boggs was only wounded in the head, and doctors say he'll live!"

The crowd cheered. Despite their disapproval of his politics, they had been highly offended at the notion of an outsider shooting their own ex-governor.

Suddenly a galloping horse approached. The crowd heard gunshots. They quickly quieted and turned to see — directly behind them on the road passing right to left — a lone horseman being chased by deputies.

"Him!" yelled the lead deputy. "He's the killer! It's Porter Rockwell!"

The crowd gasped. Porter rode right through the back of them, kicking off several who tried grabbing him.

"Get him!" cried one.

"Catch him! Lynch him!" shouted others.

Porter beat off with his heel the last man to grab him. The fellow flew back and knocked down three others, bowling them over like pins on a New England bowling green. Porter then took off in a dead heat for the woods a half mile distant. Once there, he figured he'd lose all pursuers in the forest.

The six deputies on his tail were slowed by the mob, but soon 12 horsemen from the crowd joined them.

Turning a sharp corner past Boggs' house, Porter rode at full gallop. Flying around another corner he dashed for the trees.

The posse closed in. All 18 horsemen caught sight of him disappearing around another corner two blocks ahead, and split up to trap him.

Porter glanced back just in time to discern the trap. He jumped his horse over a wall surrounding a manor and quickly dismounted. He snuck beside the horse to the edge of the property, separated from the now halting mob only by the one foot thickness of the five foot high stone wall and eight foot high hedge. The people inside the manor had evidently retired as all lights were extinguished.

Porter heard his horse grunt, and quietened it.

From the other side of the wall he heard half the horsemen coming to a halt at his left, while the other half approached from the right. This was the intersection at which they'd hoped to intercept him.

"Where's he at?"

"'He a phantom or what?"

Suddenly a woman inside caught sight of him and began banging her window at him, wanting him to get off her property. He tried shushing her, but to no avail. Then she spotted the posse over the wall and tried yelling for help, figuring Porter a fugitive. The sheriff heard the muffled screams. "What's that!"

Completely disconcerted by what they saw next, the posse spotted Porter leaping the wall on horseback. He sailed right over them and, with his momentum, soon jumped to a full block lead on them.

Two possemen galloping behind fired from horseback.

Porter turned another corner and there it lay . . . the thick forest right outside Independence. He shot straight for the trees. The mob pursued, but not fast enough. They saw him disappear. They halted.

"What're you waiting for?" shouted the sheriff. "Head in after him!"

"Them's thick woods, sheriff," said the lead deputy.

"Shut up and stay on his tail."

All 18 horsemen rode with the sheriff into the woods.

Surprised to find he was still being followed, Porter ducked a tree limb and rode deeper into the trees. A half minute later he heard a whack! followed by an "Ow!" and then a thud. The woods were taking its toll. He heard another yelp, and another thud.

He smiled, and kept riding.

Deeper into the woods he maneuvered his roan.

A mile later he heard the horsemen arguing among themselves, and then he heard a gunshot. The sheriff was attempting to regain authority, but to no avail. The horsemen had decided to retreat from the eery, fog-shrouded woods. Owls and night creatures concerned the men, frightening many, and the closer they approached the city, the faster they retreated.

Porter smiled broader as he headed eastward toward Nauvoo but, in his smile, was the shadow of agony.

He continued Eastward, determined to see if Joseph had escaped the bounty-hunters.

His journey ate at his emotions until he felt gaunt, but then he took heart — in the night-shrouded spring woodlands through which he traveled — of reuniting with his mother and siblings and with Joseph. Although he was embarrassed at the explanations he'd have to offer of his empty-handed return —

leaving his family in Missouri — he would be returning to the land where he was loved, wanted and respected.

Making his way with head bent low and hat pulled over his head, he traveled eastward.

He had ridden three hours through thick woods when he came to the main road leading East from Independence. He stopped and gazed at the road toward Nauvoo. Certainly Joseph was in danger, but Porter's children were defenseless and through the years could be poisoned against him. As torn as he felt, he fully realized he was at another crucial crossroads in his life, figuratively and literally. He could turn left for Nauvoo or right to return to Independence. Images of his family, precious Emily, and the younger children beckoned him. But so did thoughts of helping his mother, his younger siblings, and Joseph. He turned his horse to the left and rode eastward toward Nauvoo. Then stopped. He turned his horse around. And decided he would have to get his family or die trying.

CHAPTER 17

Porter figured few would see him riding through Independence in the middle of the night. Certainly none would suspect such gall. And no one would recognize him in the dark.

A half hour later, snow began falling heavily as he re-entered town. The place was asleep. He kept his hat low, detouring around the merchant district and riding through perfectly quiet residential streets. One horseman came from a side road and passed him.

"Evening," said Porter.

"Evening," said the horseman, looking suspiciously at him but riding on.

Porter wondered if the rider recognized him. He glanced back but the man was gone, already concealed from visibility by the falling snow. It had come suddenly. From full moon to snow storm. He was soon a half mile out of town, half way to Luana's parents. He quickly thought of a strategy.

As he approached Luana's farmhouse he recalled deeper memories, stirred by the whirling snowflakes.

He remembered his honeymoon dance beside the river he so loved.

He stopped 30 yards from her parents' porch. Peering through the falling snow at the dimly lit windows he perceived the figure of a woman, and discerned her kissing the children goodnight. She blew out a candle.

Porter snuck through the open front door — since it was common to leave cabins unlocked — and he walked slowly through the front room where the children stayed. He reached over and, from the dim light beaming through the window, he discovered little sleeping Orrin DeWitt, his son of 3 1/2 years, and kissed him. Then he caressed Caroline's cheek, and finally he found Emily. His heart pounded. He kissed her — and she awakened. Porter placed his hand over her mouth and she silently shouted with glee. When she settled down, Porter removed his hand and hugged her.

He then caught sight of a lantern's light reflecting off the walls. He darted to the doorway leading to the next room. He leaned back in order to not be seen when the light cascaded into the children's room.

He beheld Luana, then he stepped into the light. Luana saw him and gasped.

He shut the door behind him. Luana realized she was cut off from her parents.

"What the devil!" she whispered.

"Alive and in person."

"What're you doing?"

"Still searching for that answer."

"Pa and Ma will get you killed."

"I don't think so."

Suddenly the door burst open and Luana screamed.

CHAPTER 18

Luana's father stood in the framework holding a shotgun. Porter jerked to the side and lunged in a flash behind him, then grabbed him.

"Drop it!" said Porter.

"Never."

Porter choked him, his forearm across the man's throat. "I said drop it."

Losing his wind, Isaac Beebe dropped the gun. Porter grabbed it before it hit the floor, and in one motion released him and whirled the gun up, pointing it at him. With his foot Porter was about to slam the door when Luana's mother came groggily into the room to inspect the noise.

"Well, it looks like we're all one big happy family again," said Porter, "don't it?"

Olive Beebe gaped at him.

Porter kept the gun on her husband. Olive shifted her gaze to the gun.

"What do you want with us?" said Olive.

"To stay out of the way."

"Is this your idea," said Luana loudly, "of forcing people's wills once again?"

"I happen to love you and the kids, but I'm giving you a choice. I'll finish out my job training Ward's horses, and if you decide at that time to stay here or come with me, I won't force you either way. I just want you to give me a chance."

Luana silently sighed.

He descried within her eyes a glimmer of concern and trust.

"All right," she finally replied. "If you see I have no love for you, then you will go back alone."

"Fair enough," he said.

"Likely it's the last you'll ever see of her," said Olive, "after I get the deputies again."

"Mama," said Luana, "we won't do that. We've made a deal. For my sake, let's get along. Then he'll see his mistake."

"But I can't trust you to not see the sheriff again and set another trap," said Porter to Olive. "So I'm taking Luana and the kids to live with me at Ward's place for insurance." He glared at Olive. "You don't want gunplay around your grandkids, do ya?"

Olive studied him without responding.

"If you get the sheriff to come out there," said Porter, "then I'll take your daughter back to Nauvoo for sure — even against her will."

"No, Porter, my parents won't interfere."

"You agree to this nonsense?" said Olive.

"Yes," said Luana, "and so will you."

Olive studied her daughter's eyes, and finally melted.

"All right, you can trust us," said Olive.

"Where will they live — in some barn?" said Isaac.

"In the house with Ward and me," said Porter. He's a widower."

"This is outrageous!" said Isaac.

"Pa," said Luana, "We must do it. Then he'll be gone for good." She turned to Porter. "Is that the deal?"

"That's the deal. You'll have your freedom to choose, but I will show you that you and the kids should stay with me."

Luana and her parents glanced at each other then back at Porter.

At Cyrus Ward's farm Porter worked the horses, when suddenly both men heard the wail of a one year old baby. Little Sarah Jane was unhappy and Luana could not quieten her. Olive had just helped Luana and the children move into Ward's large cabin. She and Luana were surprised to find Porter entering the house from the corral.

Porter took the blanket-wrapped baby and held her to his chest and smiled broadly. "Sarah," he said, "my how I feel I've always known and loved you." He held the baby securely and she ceased crying.

Olive studied him, and for an instant, for the first time ever, she almost admired him.

At Ward's home the three youngest Rockwell children napped while Emily performed chores. Luana stood at the doorway and studied Porter working the corral. Cyrus Ward was congenial and gave them the entire house in which to live except for his own small bedroom where he could read each night. He joined them only for meals which Luana cooked — but for which he supplied the food — as the trade-off for allowing them to stay at his home. Luana found their landlord a gracious host.

Porter was another matter. He and Luana were frustrated over the uncertainty of their future together, and she found him moodier than normal, yet realized he made concerted efforts to be attentive to her. She simply did not know where to go from here.

Three days later on Sunday she discovered him reading the *Bible* and *Book of Mormon*. She sensed his frustration at having no church to attend. By late afternoon she found herself perceiving him in a different light. She admired his devotion to their faith. She felt a certain remorse that she did not hold to their precepts with such conviction as she once had. It began gnawing at her. When they went to bed that night he fell quickly asleep, but she continued reading in a chair. She blew out the candle and laid beside him, then felt a strange sensation. She slid out of bed, onto her knees. She felt an overwhelming presence beckoning her to reconsider her life and its direction. Tears streamed down her face. She thought she could not live with Porter and the loneliness he imposed on her, but she also felt compelled to take certain steps in other matters. With her family asleep she arose, strode to the doorway and slipped into the chilled, spring evening air with a blanket over her shoulders. She walked to the corral, leaned against the fence and simply gazed off at the moon. She knew with a clarity what she would do the next morning.

At her parents' home she entered, sat and, with a contriteness not characteristic of her, faced her father and mother.

"Well?" said Olive, seated beside her husband Isaac on the sofa opposite their daughter.

"I've watched him five years, often out of the corner of my eye."

"And?"

"He's deserted me for another."

"Another?" said Olive.

"Adventure."

"We all know that, Luana. So, what have you decided?"

"I've decided on the other hand he's quite an example of faith and devotion which I haven't consistently had."

"What're you saying?" said her father bruskly.

"I've still got my eye on things."

"After all he's put you through," said Olive, "that's all you can sit here and say?"

"No. Despite his faults, I've decided to return to Nauvoo."

"I cannot believe," said Olive, "you are saying this. Don't you know what to do with your life? Haven't we taught you since a little girl how to make the right choices?"

"Exactly that," said Luana. "And what I've decided is because of my love for you."

"This is certainly a warped way of looking at us loving you," said Olive.

"First, I have to confess I feel ashamed for my rebellious-ness to you my whole life."

"You've been a near-perfect daughter," said Isaac.

"I've rebelled quietly. And that's why I married Porter, in part. I rebelled in subtle ways against other things you taught me. Ironically, that helped me stay active in the faith. But I am so sorry I gave you a hard time growing up. I suppose my re-belliousness transferred, when I married. And in my heart for awhile I fought Joseph, as a way of fighting Porter. But I'm not here to talk about that. I have indeed felt deserted by Porter and I'll deal with that later. But I am truly . . . " She stopped. Tears welled in her eyes.

" . . . sorry for things."

"What things?" said Olive.

"My heart not being in the faith. Not trying. I don't want to slide anymore. I can't. I've thought hard about this. I cannot desert what I know to be true. I know Joseph is the Prophet of the Lord. I've decided to rejoin activity full force. And I know . . . in order for us all to live together . . . with you two people who mean more to me, with my children, than anyone in the world . . . that you must rejoin me in the faith so we can all live together in the next life. That's the only way we can."

Both her parents sat there, surprised but not entirely dis-mayed. They thoughtfully considered her words, in silence. Finally her father spoke:

"We hope you'll be happy in your faith and in Illinois."

Luana smiled a painful smile and arose, then walked several feet to their sofa, knelt, and gave them each a kiss. Tears flowed down her cheeks. Without another word, she arose and left.

As the Rockwell family packed the wagon outside Ward's cabin, preparing to return to Nauvoo, Porter felt an overwhelming gratitude for having his prayers answered. Luana had made it clear she was undecided about their marriage, but at least he was getting his family home to Nauvoo — and she had told him of her renewed desire to be active in the faith.

He suddenly realized he was being watched. He looked up and Cyrus Ward was scrutinizing him.

"I've appreciated your hospitality," said Porter.

Ward seemed lost in thought.

Porter wondered how much Ward knew; in any case he felt guilty over his cover-up, and sensed Ward could see straight through him. Porter leaned back on his wagon in order to relax and feel more confidence.

"I gotta confess something."

Ward analyzed him harder, studying his eyes.

"My name is not 'Brown,'" said Porter.

"What is it?"

"Porter Rockwell."

"*The* Porter Rockwell?"

Porter nodded.

Ward smiled. "I've never had a celebrity visit, much less live here."

"Some celebrity," Porter snorted.

"Celebrity, nonetheless. I've got to tell you I haven't approved of Boggs, or especially the way he treated you people when he was governor. On top of that he put the state in a real bind. 'Lot of folks think he had that shot coming to him."

"He seems popular to a lot of others," said Porter, referring to the mob that chased him through town.

"So," said Ward, staring at his face, "did you shoot him?"

Porter had never actually denied the shooting to Luana, he had merely registered surprise when she had accused him. Now he merely stared at Ward, but in that gaze Cyrus had his answer.

"Your eyes don't lie," said Ward.

"So what's your verdict?"

"You and I both know."

CHAPTER 19

The May sunshine of 1842 drenched Porter's senses. Riding home to Nauvoo with his family, he invented a plan: If any horsemen happened to ride past, he would jump off the wagon and dash for the woods. The second part of "the plan" was for Luana to yell at him for having to urinate so frequently since he'd gotten drunk. She laughed over his strategm, but agreed.

Not three hours into their ride, several miles east of Independence, they approached two riders. Porter spotted them, turned his head in order to not be recognized, and jumped down from the buckboard. Luana parroted her agreed line of dialogue, and Porter shouted back from the cover of trees:

"Shut up, woman. When you gotta go, etcetera!"

The horsemen chuckled and kept riding.

Later that afternoon Porter, riding beside Luana, glanced at her to determine her feelings. She seemed at ease about going to Nauvoo, but would not discuss anything further.

"Feels good riding as a family," Porter offered.

"We're fortunate to have good weather," she replied, evading the issue.

Luana held little Sarah on the buckboard, and before sunset she was surprised by Porter breaking into children's folk songs. Immediately the older children jumped in singing. Luana found it entertaining the first 20 minutes; two hours later she was annoyed beyond distraction.

"I think we're deep into twilight now," she said, attempting to stop his singing, "so we better camp down."

"No, I'll make a couple torches. That way we can keep riding. The weather's warm and we'll make it there sooner."

"How can you see where we're going even now?" said Luana.

"I reckon I can follow anything in moonlight. 'Probably comes from Pa's line of the family. He could do the same and so could his pa. We used to 'possum hunt in Manchester, and when they had contests I could track them at night better than anyone."

"Not bad for a 14 year old," said Luana.

"I was six."

Luana never ceased to be amazed by his uncanny wilderness skills. She knew he had won every shooting contest he had entered since he was 10. But this was additional news.

"I suppose," she summarized, "you're just a born adventurer."

"I reckon."

In the rising moon she glanced at him beside her and in his eyes she caught from the label, "adventurer" a sparkling glint of pride.

"That's what I'm afraid of," she said.

CHAPTER 20

Arriving at the Mississippi, Porter smiled broadly. It was the first major landmark of home, and always made his spirit celebrate. He loved this wide, powerful river.

Luana looked upon it with apprehension. She would have to make a decision on their marriage soon, and if she decided to part ways with Porter, she would be having to face the pressure and embarrassment of her situation with friends and neighbors. She knew her homecoming to Nauvoo and her recommitment to spiritual values was the right decision, she was merely distressed over the potential pain she would have to socially endure.

Entering their neighborhood, Luana insisted Porter stay with his mother, while she and the children live separately from him. Disappointed, he complied.

"Only till we work out a solution," she said.

Porter felt a cautious hope.

Living at Sarah's home, the dog Ugly was surprised when Porter asked:

"Mind if I sleep in your bed, boy?"

The dog was gracious and even seemed pleased to have him climb in his bed.

Ugly would fall asleep every night with his nozzle on Porter's chest. The dog was in heaven. At dinner, however, all was not bliss. After several days Porter's brother Peter expressed concern over his brother's view of farm work:

"It's good, honest labor, you know," said Peter. "If you tried it harder you might see smoother sailing in the future."

Porter arose without a word and went outside. He could hear all his brothers launching into an argument until he was out of hearing range: Horace supported Porter's desire for a free-er lifestyle, the other two did not. Their mother finally interceded. "It's really not anybody's business."

He spent the day walking through her mother's farm acreage on the East end of town, kicking an occasional dirt clod, and thinking. While feeling a measured hope of living again with his wife and kids, he felt frustrated things were not progressing faster.

At night he seemed less morose, and his mother was careful to keep the dinner conversation on relatively safe topics such as the city's growing-pains, the neighbors, and old friends.

"Mayor Bennett was excommunicated," she said.

"What?"

"He was moving through a few bedrooms about town — quite a charmer he was — when Joseph caught up to him. Bennett was mad as a plucked chicken, and he resigned as mayor." That had been several days earlier on May 17, 1842.

"Why don't you see Joseph now?" said Sarah. "You know he's been worried about you."

Porter was embarrassed to report his marriage problems to his best friend. The topic would be unavoidable since Joseph would undoubtedly ask about his welfare.

"Yeah." He retired to bed, drained.

Just before sundown his mother awakened him from a nap and reminded him of the town meeting. She told him to go and get his mind off Luana.

He cleaned, ate a quick supper, prepared his horse, and rode off first to see Joseph. Riding across town he observed the beauty of the city:

The initial homes built had been simple log cabins, until lumber was sent down river from Wisconsin. This lumber allowed more elaborate homes to be constructed, such as his parents'. There were numerous streets neatly laid out and by now filled with homes — about 1200 log cabins, over 300 frame houses and over 200 brick homes. The saints were now making their own brick. Those inhabitants from New York mostly built Greek Revival style houses — with specific types of columns, pilasters and simple moldings — a style which swept the U.S. as the most popular style of the day, while immigrants from New England leaned toward the Federal style — with its square shapes, arched entrances, horizontal siding, and fan and triple windows. Other homes in the city had mixed styles. Brick homes usually had gabled roofs and boxed shapes with chimneys at the ends — often double chimneys.

As Porter rode down the hill toward Joseph's "Homestead," he recalled recent winters where Joseph had taught his children to slide downhill on the ice, balancing themselves. He had also shown them how to sleigh downhill and out onto the frozen river. (Author's note: These were actual, little-known activities Joseph taught his children, according to a primary historical source.)

Porter approached Joseph's home. He found the structure unique: Originally it was only a log cabin built in 1803 and used as the first Indian agency in Illinois. Joseph moved into it May 10, 1839. But in 1840 he attached a frame house to it.

He was currently building a new home called the Mansion House up the street which would be completed the following year, in 1843, but he planned to keep utilizing the Homestead for family members.

In the wooden frame add-on to the Homestead was the secret hiding room made of brick, located under the stairway which led to the cellar. It held two people, and Joseph would use it several times over the years when hunted by enemies.

Riding through Nauvoo Porter enjoyed the sight and feel of the city — the 50 foot wide streets and eight foot wide sidewalks, with three larger streets possessing even wider sidewalks. All the homes were a specific distance from the road and attractively landscaped with plants, shrubbery, and trees. Some roads were paved with gravel, while sidewalks consisted of stone, gravel, or brick.

The place was stunning.

That spring, on April 16, 1842, an interesting newspaper began — different from most others of its day. *The Wasp* was edited by Joseph's younger brother, William, whom Porter found at times cantankerous and generally not as supportive to Joseph as his other siblings, yet all were pleased with the paper, which covered some news but mostly art, literature, trading, business, and farming — a very practical and interesting publication. It also answered anti-church articles from other, nearby newspapers. Porter had his friends and family read it aloud to him each week while he, like the rest of the city, waited excitedly for each issue when it would fly hot off the press.

The other Nauvoo newspaper, *Times and Seasons,* concerned itself with the development and expansion of the church. It also published a lengthy article series written by Joseph giving background to their history as well as the backdrop to his prophetic declarations, the revelations he felt were given him from God. The newspaper was, interestingly, not a religious one. And there had been several predecessors.

Porter also took note of a "photography shop" in town, set up by Lucian Foster, the first man to photograph Nauvoo. This man also possibly made a "daguerreotype" of Joseph.

Nauvoo was a beaming "city on a hill," and was quite a sight for the over-200 steamboats operating the Mississippi River.

Riding downhill to the Homestead Porter noticed a sizeable crowd gathered. He spotted Joseph in the fading orange light of dusk, standing on his stately lawn, fifteen feet in front of the doorway.

"Brothers and Sisters, you should know we just received word that Lilburn W. Boggs, former governor of Missouri, has been shot in an assassination attempt. As you know, I have preached publicly and prayed privately that — although Mr.

Boggs has caused untold suffering to our people — we want him to live because, if he were to leave this life in his current state, I would fear for his soul. Any feelings or attitudes of celebration are entirely out of the bounds of propriety. We further understand that he seems to be recovering well, and should live."

Porter wondered if Boggs deserved to live, given Joseph's perspective. He then caught sight of John Cook Bennett.

Bennett saw him and glanced away, then disappeared in the dust of the crowd and made his way up street. Porter still felt awkward explaining his domestic problems to Joseph, so he avoided him.

The next several weeks went slowly. Porter worked full days on the farm and spent his evenings in solitude. He would visit the children at noon "dinner" and listen to Emily tell of her day. It pained him to see Luana's alternating coldness and warmth, and to miss the evenings with his children. Finally, he confronted her:

"How do you see things now?"

She understood what he meant. After putting dishes away she turned, folded her arms, and faced him.

"You've certainly been more attentive to the children."

"And?"

"I like that," she said.

He saw a smile gleaming behind her eyes. He hoped it was indicative of their reuniting. She was still reconsidering their relationship, but was uncertain. While he was hopeful she wanted him back, what he actually read were mere feelings for him— and there was a distinct difference.

"Are you ready for me to make the move?" he said.

"Maybe," she smiled. "But you are welcome to join us for all your meals, and spend as much time here as you like."

"I suppose with you," he said, "is what you mean."

She again smiled. "I mean the children, but as time goes on, we'll see." She could not mask the increasing interest she felt re-developing in her heart. "Right now," she added, "we need supplies from the general store." She handed him a list. "Can you get these, if we can afford them?"

He knew they could — he was having a good summer selling early produce from the fields. He smiled at her and, like a teenager back in Independence, once outside by himself, swung his fist in the air.

Before getting the supplies, he felt like he should celebrate.

CHAPTER 21

Porter's hope and happiness was so intense that he finally wished to confide in his best friend. On a warm early July 1842 evening, he set out to see Joseph.

The Prophet was busy writing a letter to the Quincy Whig, replying to an article that claimed Joseph had predicted Boggs' death, and thus implemented him in the shooting.

Porter explained to Joseph in detail his adventure in Independence and reported that he and Luana were now living apart, but would likely be getting back together. Joseph hugged him, hopeful for him, and then at Porter's request read his newspaper letter aloud:

"You have done me manifest injustice in ascribing to me a prediction of the demise of Lilburn W. Boggs . . . Boggs was a candidate for the state senate and, I presume, fell by the hand of a political opponent . . . but he did not through my instrumentality." (Author's note: This was the actual text of the letter.)

As Joseph read, Emma entered with a grave expression and handed him another newspaper just received from a messenger. The *Sangamo Journal* reported John Bennett had come to their editor and "exposed" the Boggs assassination attempt. Joseph read the article aloud: "Smith said to me, speaking of Governor Boggs, 'The Destroying Angel has done the work, as I predicted, but Porter was not the man who shot him; the Angel did it.'"

Porter glanced at Joseph, surprised.

"So that's who told the newspapers I'd predicted Boggs' death," said Joseph. "John Bennett. He must've felt so humiliated by his excommunication that he went to the press with these absurd stories."

Joseph was soon brought another newspaper article — from the *Jefferson Republican*. He read aloud:

"'The obvious assassin is Porter Rockwell, since Joseph Smith had prophesied of Boggs' death.'"

Porter glared angrily at the paper.

"This is all fairly convenient," said Joseph. "The *Lee County Democrat* printed right after the crime that they had thoroughly investigated it and found the assassins had escaped undetected. Other newspapers said the gun used was traced to Philip Uhlinger's grocery. Still others thought a man named Tompkins shot him."

Porter shook his head.

"Any loyal friend of mine," said Joseph, "is bound to receive fire. So welcome to the embers, Porter."

Both were to soon be the target of a new wave of anti-Mormon press — that which would fuel local non-Mormons to anger and start a flood of dissension among less-committed saints. It began when the *Sangamo Journal* asked Bennett to write a series of articles to "expose" the saints. The series had begun July 1 and would continue another two months, till September 1842. Bennett would also travel locally as a lecturer against the church and publish a book condemning it. His intention — as well as those from other dissenters who suddenly emerged from obscurity — was to incite anger against Joseph and the kingdom.

The saints' political and economic power had already concerned the locals, but now with Bennett's accusations they were ready for action. Even a full-scale storm.

Porter walked quickly from Joseph's Mansion House and made his way to his mother's home where, for the first time in days, he was unable to sleep.

On the morning of July 5, 1842 he decided to hunt down John Cook Bennett himself. He first went to Bennett's old home and found it deserted. Two neighbors, Warner and Davis, sauntered out to inform him of additional claims Bennett had made to them. A tip from a third neighbor led Porter to Carthage twelve miles southeast, where the same afternoon he arrived at the hotel of Mr. Hamilton. Porter entered and saw Bennett seated with three other men.

(The following dialogue was later reported verbatim by Bennett:)

"Can I have a private interview with you?" said Porter.

"If you have anything to say, speak out before the gentlemen present," said Bennett.

"It's a private matter."

Bennett simply gazed at him.

"Doctor," said Porter, "You do not know your friends; I am not your enemy, and I do not wish you to make use of my name in your publications."

"I recognize Joe Smith and all his friends as my personal enemies."

"I have been informed,"said Porter, "by Warner and Davis that you said Joseph gave me fifty dollars and a wagon for shooting Boggs, and I can and will whip any man that will tell such a lie; did you say so or not?"

Bennett studied him a moment. "I never said so, sir, but I did say, and I now say it to your face, that you left Nauvoo about two months before the attempted assassination of Ex-Governor Boggs of Missouri and returned the day before the report of his assassination reached there; and that two persons in Nauvoo told me that you told them that you had been over the upper part of Missouri and in Boggs' neighborhood."

"Well I was there," said Porter. "And if I shot Boggs they have got to prove it. I never did an act in my life that I was ashamed of, and I do not fear to go anywhere that I have ever been. I have done nothing criminal."

"Certainly they have got to prove it on you, if you did shoot him," said Bennett. "I know nothing of what you did, as I was not there. I only know the circumstances, and from them I draw my own inferences, and the public will theirs, and now, sir, if either you or Joe Smith think you can intimidate me by your threats, you are mistaken in your man, and I wish you to understand distinctly that I am opposed to Joe and his holy host. I shall tell the truth fearlessly, regardless of consequences."

"If you say that Joseph gave me fifty dollars and a wagon to shoot Boggs, I can whip you, and will do it in any crowd."

"Why are you harping on what I have not said?" said Bennett. "I have told you what I have said, to your face, and in the presence of these gentlemen, and you have acknowledged the truth of all I have said, and I'll say it again; and if you wish to fight, I am ready for you."

"I've been accused wrongfully of wishing to assassinate him, or of being ordered by Joseph to do so."

"Well I believe Joe ordered you to do it."

"Joseph never gave me any such orders, neither was it his intention."

Porter left the four men and blustered outside into a hot evening breeze, red with frustration.

Ten days later the *Sangamo Journal* reported that Porter killed a Mormon in Nauvoo — a man named John Stephenson. It was the second murder accusation he had received, and both within so short a time, he mused, that he must be on his way to outlaw stardom.

The thought immediately occurred to him what Luana must

be thinking — and what she might tell the children. His frustration forced him to walk to the Mississippi and pace its banks. An hour later he strode to Joseph's Homestead.

"Joseph, I can't work the fields any more — I need something different to work at."

"I don't mean to sound cold, old friend, but sometimes we have to bare with our trials. I'd like to help you but can't afford to hire you for anything."

"I didn't expect that, but don't you know any other work around?"

"I'm sorry I don't," said Joseph. "But you could pray for strength to endure, like the Nephite prisoners did. Their account in the *Book of Mormon* was of the Lamanite guards holding them captive and putting heavy burdens on their backs. So when the Nephites plead to the Lord, he made the burdens lighter."

Porter's plight was two-fold: Not only did he wish for different work, he did not know how to handle the Stephenson murder news with Luana. Thus, he wanted to avoid it altogether.

Joseph sensed that and confronted him. "It's really her, isn't it?"

Porter nodded.

"Just tell her the truth."

"She's so afraid what others think," said Porter, "that I don't know how to . . . You weren't at my wedding, but at the Big Blue and other times since . . . well . . . I'm just worried what she's thinking on this Boggs and Stephenson stuff in the press."

"You'll never know until you see her," said Joseph.

His younger friend just stared at him.

CHAPTER 22

Porter was right. Luana would hardly talk to him, confused and torn.

"Luana, I did not do it."

"I think I believe you."

"What do you mean 'think?'"

"I also think you're capable," she said.

"Why?"

"Your threats — your father's death."

"So what do *you* really think?" he said.

"I think . . . " she paused. "I think I'm right — you're innocent."

"Then that's all that matters."

As she watched him walk out the door to retrieve fruit from the porch, she muttered to herself, "I suppose."

Emily overheard, and walked into the front room. "I believe him. He's my pa and that's all that matters."

Luana gazed at her a moment and shook her head. "I suppose that's true." Nevertheless, Luana was concerned what the public thought as reflected in the newspapers, yet she was simultaneously charmed by him as he returned into the cabin and bellowed out with a broad smile:

"Of course she's right."

Luana fought a smile. "Well are you staying for dinner?"

Porter put his arm across Emily's shoulders and said, "You couldn't talk me out of it!"

Emily giggled as Porter picked her up and swung her.

For an instant, Luana felt jealousy, but buried it.

Days later Porter again stopped to see Joseph, this time with news he had learned outside the saddle shop. It was just after sunset and the colors were a soft hue. He was invited by Emma into Joseph's study.

"Bennett has gone to see Lilburn Boggs," Porter blurted.

Joseph looked off contemplatively.

Porter continued, "I overheard visitors who were touring the city. They said Boggs was recuperating in Independence. And that Bennett had found him at home. Bennett supposedly told him about your hiring me — his usual story. And I guess Boggs believed him. Boggs then swore out an affidavit to arrest us."

Joseph sighed. "Boggs would have to petition the Governor of Illinois first. I don't know if Carlin would comply. Missouri and Illinois have bad blood between them — including their state officials. I think we're safe here."

"I don't know."

More days passed. Porter wondered if and when the Boggs affidavit would become public. He worried over what Luana's reaction would be.

On August 8, 1842 Porter noticed several people gathered on Joseph's front lawn. As he rode closer he realized they were two lawmen with badges interrogating Joseph and the Nauvoo city marshal. He overheard one of the deputies accusing Joseph and shouting at him. He trotted up quickly and dismounted, then strode up to the deputy and shoved his shoulder.

The deputy lost his balance and fell to the road. He pulled out a pistol, but Porter kicked it away.

Then Porter bellowed, "If you got any more questions, talk to me."

The other, heavy-set deputy jumped in Porter's face. "Who do you think you are, talking to us like that?"

"I'm Porter Rockwell, and I talk to any man as I please."

The stouter deputy studied Porter's eyes of steel. His own eyes suddenly widened. "You're Orrin Porter Rockwell?"

The thinner deputy squealed boldly, "I don't care who you are. You're up for a night in jail for pushing my partner!"

"If you take me to jail, only one of us would reach that place alive."

"Is that a threat?" said the thin deputy.

Porter smiled, "I suppose you could call it that."

The stouter deputy's mouth quivered. He tried shushing his partner. Then spoke in hushed tones, "Don't you remember that name, stupid?"

"What was that?" squealed the taller one.

"Porter . . . Rockwell. The wanted posters?"

The thin deputy's long, skinny face suddenly went white.

Joseph broke in, "Porter, these gentlemen are deputies from Missouri. Governor Carlin has complied with Mr. Boggs' request, and it seems I'm under arrest."

The thin deputy's voice squealed like a stuck pig. "You too, Mr. Rockwell!"

Porter's voice went calm and cool, "Nobody's touching me." He then pulled up his pistol and pointed it at the thin deputy.

Joseph held up both palms towards him:

"It's all right, Porter. Brother Markham is bringing a little document that will change things. Put that away, please."

The two deputies regarded Porter fearfully, until he put away his pistol. Then all immediately noticed Markham galloping up to them.

"Mister," said the thin deputy turning to Joseph, "What're you talking about — what document?"

"I think you'll be heading back to Missouri alone," said Joseph, smiling "Let me have that paper, Stephen."

Markham handed it to Joseph from horseback.

Joseph held it out to the two deputies. "This little paper is called a *writ of habeas corpus.* What it does is keep us in Nauvoo, and I'm afraid under the law you can't take us out."

The thin deputy snarled at Joseph, grabbing his arm. Porter elbowed the deputy in the stomach, and the lawman keeled over, releasing Joseph. "I think," said Porter, "the law is on our side. If you want to face me two on one, give me your best shot. Otherwise, get out of our town or I'll drag you across the river myself!"

The stouter deputy quivered again, then grabbed his partner's arm and said, "Let's go."

When they got to their horses, they glowered back at Porter. The slimmer one forced a smile. "We'll see who wins out, Mr. Rockwell. We'll see." He spat on the ground towards Porter, then both men took off in a gallop.

Joseph blew out a sigh and turned to Porter:

"I'll be in hiding awhile till this blows over, and I suggest you get busy gardening your mother's property east of town and keep yourself low and out of sight." Joseph then patted him on the shoulder. "Thanks, Porter. You're ever at my defense, aren't you?"

Porter beamed.

As they parted, Porter realized he would indeed have to spend his time at his mother's garden, but at dark could sneak through less-used paths to visit his children and Luana. He knew the Stephenson murder publicity still weighed on his wife, and that she would remain torn over how to deal with him. It bothered him how she still cared so much what other people think. Especially strangers. He took it as a personal blow that she would both concern herself with the assumptions of others and that she could even in the slightest manner doubt his trustworthiness. Trusting others—especially men — had always seemed an issue with her. He couldn't understand it.

Three days after he had parted with Joseph, he decided to visit Luana and the children, unable to stay away any longer.

He left his mother's garden after dark, passing three Missouri bounty hunters who were riding horseback through the streets. He turned his face in order to not be recognized. One of the riders glanced at him suspiciously but, not fully discerning his face in the darkness, kept riding the opposite direction.

Arriving at Luana's cabin, Porter was surprised to be met with a hug from Luana. The children were asleep in the bedroom, except for Emily, who was thrilled to see him, yet was tired and yawning.

"I think I've got nine lives," said Porter after he told her of the strangers he had barely evaded.

"Like a cat?" said Luana.

"Like a mountain lion," quipped Emily, proudly.

Luana and Porter laughed. Porter's hope was soaring and he grinned.

"I think," said Luana, becoming suddenly serious, "despite the danger, you should leave after supper and go see Joseph. He could probably use this sack of cakes and muffins I baked today," she added, pulling them out. Emma was over earlier, and gave me this map to give you. It shows the island in the river where Joseph is staying. He's expecting you. Stay with him as many days as you need," she said. "I support you completely."

He looked at her curiously. "You just want to get me shot," he smiled.

She smiled back, but was serious:

"I just want you to help your friend. His life is in the greatest danger it's probably ever been in, and he needs our help. I suspect he needs your friendship, especially."

Porter was taken back by her cooperative spirit. It was so dramatically different from her earlier battles she had launched whenever he wished to see Joseph, that it disconcerted him.

"And I have other news for you," she said. "My parents are moving here — they sold their farm and will buy a small one here." Tears glistened in her eyes. "They want to re-activate in the faith."

Porter felt genuinely happy for her. He also gazed at her appreciatively, feeling the greatest optimism yet over their future life together.

He could now see himself raising his children. He pulled Emily close, and hugged her hard. She kissed her father, yawned silently, and disappeared into the bedroom to sleep. His heart pounded with hope.

"Porter," said Luana, "I have other news for you. And this is not so good. When Emma Smith came by today, she told me this — For some reason, you and Joseph will have to leave the city for several months."

A sudden realization hit him like an agonizing sickness in the pit of his soul.

CHAPTER 23

This was possibly, he suspected, the defining moment of his life, where all his struggles, pain and frustration had brought him, and he realized that the next several moments would determine the outcome of his most heart-wrenching concerns — whether or not he actually could raise his children and keep Luana and the four little ones.

He went to the children's bedroom and picked up Emily, then baby Sarah, Caroline, and Orrin DeWitt, with tears welling. After 20 minutes he returned to the front room. Luana had never seen him so distressed.

"You've become a celebrity," she said, trying to ease the tension.

"If you want to call it that."

"I heard the news," she added. "A neighbor showed me a newspaper."

"About Boggs or Stephenson?"

"Both."

"I was afraid the Stephenson news would hit the papers sooner or later," he said. "We've already been through this Boggs thing. Can't we move on?"

"I suppose," she said, "but within the week both stories will be in every newspaper in the territory."

"I reckon," he frowned. "And I'm sorry you care so all-fired much what they think."

"All I know is the children must be raised right."

"That's why I want to raise them."

"They must be free from people looking down their noses at them as kids of a common criminal," she said.

"So what in tarnation is common about my criminal reputation?" he said.

She smiled.

"He got serious. Nobody knows who I am out of Illinois, Iowa and Missouri, and none of this Boggs and Stephenson stuff has probably even gotten to the papers anywhere else. So I want you to come with me."

"What're you talking about?"

"Leave the state with me."

Luana sat down, the wind all but knocked out of her:

"Such another pilgrimage would be quite impossible for a family, don't you think?"

"We took on Missouri together."

"With all your shooting contest earnings and all our savings. Now we're broke, and if our wagon broke on another journey, or our food got bugs, we'd be stuck up a creek, wouldn't we?"

"Then we'd settle there," said Porter, "while I worked and

got what we needed to move on."

"You're not realistic, Porter. Bounty hunters are all over the place."

"You'll always see me as unrealistic. I'm just trying to keep my family together."

"This is not the way to do it. You're asking too much of me."

"Keeping the family together is asking too much?"

"Under these circumstances, yes," she said.

He whirled on her. "Maybe you should keep us a family for once!"

"While you're a fugitive from justice?"

"How can you look at me as an outlaw? I didn't do anything!"

"Your wanting to fight enemies at every turn is hardly not doing anything," she said. "You've brought this all on yourself; can't you see that?"

"What if I have," he said. "Ain't it your responsibility to stick by me?"

"Only to the point of reasonableness. And I will not gallivant across the countryside with a suspected criminal. Your ideas are outrageous!"

"Then I'll have to go it alone — without my wife's support?"

"It's a little late to be playing the martyr here, don't you think?"

"I'm just telling you the truth," he said, beginning to pack gear that he kept at her cabin.

"Porter . . . " Luana glanced down. "Sooner or later somebody will recognize you — and you'll be arrested or killed. And now I'm telling you the truth."

"Not in another territory."

"I can't accept having to await the awful news — and for the children to learn — whether you're dead or captured. That's too much of a strain for me."

"So you just want me away from my children," said Porter. "That solves everything."

"You've proven you're not a fair-weather soldier. Washington would've been proud to have you in his army. But for me, the war is simply over."

He felt destroyed. "Then you've decided about us." he said.

She looked away, and nodded.

Porter gazed at Luana and slowly shook his head in disbelief. The flame of hope he'd felt minutes earlier was thoroughly extinguished. His soul had never before felt so darkened. His eyes caught Emily still asleep in the kids' room. He walked slowly to her, knelt at her side, and placed his face beside her. A tear crossed from his cheek to hers. She never stirred. He again kissed the others. He trod to the doorway and turned. Taking in the scene of his precious family, he knew he would remember this mental image forever. He gazed again at Luana.

She studied him, her eyes glistening, then glanced away.

When he went outside, he heard her call after him. He turned and beheld her in the framework.

"When you get back," she said, "you can visit the kids as often as you like. I want you to help raise them if you wish. They need the love of their papa — especially one who loves them as much as you."

Although he knew it would not be the same as living there, he felt nonetheless relieved.

"Providing, of course," she added, "your life is no longer in danger from the wanted posters, and it's safe for the kids to see you."

"It may never be."

She began back-tracking, "Otherwise, you could sneak here like you have been, and that's a respectable way for them to deal with you the rest of their lives, isn't it?" she smiled. "Even so, although it's not the safest world of them, they do need the love you have."

"As I need their's," he smiled in return.

"I'm certain there will be no other men in my life, in case you're wondering," she added.

"I was, because you are a beautiful woman."

She blushed slightly. "Nevertheless, no one will want to be enslaved with a grouchy, critical wife like me and all these children."

"I can't argue that," he smirked.

"You could've unloaded another compliment on me," she laughed, "such as, 'But dear, it would be an honor to be enslaved by you and a whole gaggle of kids. I couldn't wish it enough on any man.'"

"Sure," he said. "I'll say that. But I pity the poor freak it happens to." He laughed, as did she, then she started to cry simultaneously.

"It's too true, isn't it?" she said. "I'll never be loved, will I?"

He hugged her and she burst into more tears, clutching his shoulder and crying into it. He then realized for the first time, after all these years, that despite all the attention and overprotectiveness of her parents, she had never really felt loved — by them or him or anyone.

"Why don't you feel love?" he inquired.

"I don't know. Maybe I'm not worthy of it. Ever since . . ." She stopped, thinking.

"Since what?"

"Since a neighbor in New York . . . mistreated me . . . as a kid. His wife watched me during the day, when my folks were traveling a lot, looking at land and furniture to buy. Then at nights her husband would sneak in my room. I don't remember much of it or hardly any of my childhood. I guess I've blocked it out. But I've never felt right about people since. And especially about . . . me. I just wonder . . . will the hurt ever end? Will I ever feel it?"

"What?"

"Love?"

"Not the way," he said, "I have. No man could ever love another as much deep down."

"That's what I was afraid of," she laughed, again through her tears. "You're always trying to get away from me."

He didn't say it, but realized her coldness — which until now he could not understand the reason for — had played a vital part in driving him away.

She continued, smiling through her continuing tears, "With love like this from men, who needs them?"

He held her and she laughed more, while crying. She said, "You have to go now. Joseph is waiting for you. Please be safe."

He pulled away from her, turned, and began walking.

She called out, "Porter . . . "

He turned again, this time to face her.

She glued her eyes to his. "I'm sorry for the way things have worked out, honey."

He fought his own tears and turned away one final time.

CHAPTER 24

Joseph sat at a campfire on an island off the Iowa shore. He had been there three days and now stared at the vast Mississippi River. Its waves lapped gently on the bank. He was deep in thought of the moon-filled night. Presently he heard footsteps crunching across the woodland behind him. His brother Hyrum walked up, accompanied by a stranger. Shadows created by the moonlight covered the stranger's face.

Not till the stranger walked into the light of the campfire did Joseph recognize him.

"Porter!"

Joseph immediately went to him and they hugged. Several of Joseph's associates sleeping near the campfire were awakened by the commotion and arose. They all shook Porter's hand. They held him in high esteem, not only as a friend of Joseph since the beginning, but one who had never wavered when things did not go their way, as had certain of their associates from New York to Ohio to Missouri — the Harris's, Whitmers, Cowderys, and those in Missouri who had actually gone to the mobs to stir them up — although some had returned to the fold. Joseph always had forgiven them and taken them back, a trait Porter could not completely comprehend, especially in light of having witnessed his father die indirectly at the hands of the Missouri mobs.

Porter in turn held a mutual respect for these gentlemen on the island. Certainly he was the only "rough" sort among them, yet felt none of this group looked down on him. These were Joseph's closest friends; they did not include the self-prescribed intellectuals who felt superior to him. One could indeed thank Joseph for the respect Porter had within this group: Joseph obviously adored his younger friend and still considered him a younger brother to protect, howbeit that role among them in a physical sense had ironically reversed.

Sitting down at the campfire and eating jerky offered him, Porter listened to Joseph as he revealed new and secret plans to take their people to the Rocky Mountains. "The Lord has shown me the place in vision."

Porter studied the dozen men gathered about the fire. Flames flickered off their faces and he gauged their intensity.

He broke the silence in a show of verbal support.

"I'll be the first there, Joseph." He looked around. The others nodded and all eventually spoke in agreement. He then added, "How much danger are we really in, Joseph?"

"Haven't you heard?" said Joseph in amazement.

"Complete with wanted posters," said Joseph.

Porter was afraid to ask but finally did:

"For how much?"

"Fifteen hundred dollars! Each!"

Porter's eyes widened.

"Each?"

"Well . . . at least that's something my children can be proud of," chuckled Porter to himself.

"Bounty-hunters and lawmen are canvassing the city by the dozens," added Hyrum, Joseph's brother.

"So I've seen," said Porter, "but I didn't know they had so much incentive." He again sighed and added dryly, "Luana complains she don't have enough money. Maybe I could turn myself in and collect my own bounty."

Joseph chuckled, then admitted he felt distressed that he could not find sanctuary even in his own city.

Porter handed a newspaper article to Brigham Young, seated next to him. "Emma asked me to bring this for you all to read. That was my last stop before I came here." All the men were aware Porter still could not read.

Brigham quickly scanned the article and chuckled. He finally said, "This is from the *Quincy Whig*. It says two officers came searching for Joseph to arrest him but couldn't find him. Listen to this: 'The Mormons treated the officers with every respect, and offered to assist them if necessary, in fulfilling their duty. The whole affair begins to look exceedingly like a farce.'"

They all laughed.

"I can see," said Joseph, "Emma smiling when she handed that article to you, Porter."

"That, she did," said Porter. "So what're we going to do now?"

"There's only one thing to do," said Hyrum. Joseph's brother was usually quiet but managed to offer cogent advice in critical situations.

Porter looked at Hyrum, who spoke softly:

"Joseph has to stay in hiding till we get legal protection. He has to remain nearby to run the church and watch over the city. But you, Porter, must travel East. As the perceived trigger-man in all this, some spirited bounty-hunters would no doubt lynch you on the spot."

"I understand," said Porter. "But I did just bring my family back here."

Joseph broke in soberly, softly:

"He's right, Porter. You must go to Pennsylvania and stay with friends. Go to Brother and Sister Armstrong's till I notify you when it's safe to return."

Porter was distraught and gazed into the fire. The continuing idea of leaving Emily and the other children stabbed at him till he felt ill. And just when he had reached what he had hoped was a positive pinnacle in his relationship with Luana . . .

"I don't think I can go," said Porter.

"Your family," said Joseph reading his thoughts, "will have more of you if you're not dead. Even if you can't have them all."

Porter wondered on the significance of the statement. He glanced at each of their faces and realized they perceived the uselessness of the situation with Luana far more accurately than he. He suddenly realized at that moment the reality of the doom of his marriage — even if he were to stay in Nauvoo. His wants and dreams had created a fantasy of hope, which obviously only others could see. He pushed it from his mind and silently sighed, then nodded.

Joseph tried changing the subject: "I never before asked this of you, Porter, but tell me . . . I want the truth. Did you shoot him? Did you pull the trigger on Governor Boggs?"

Porter knew they were aware of his incomparable marksmanship, his uncanny skills, his irrefutable reputation with a firearm, as far back as the early shooting contests in New York.

Joseph asked him again, "Did you shoot him?"

Porter arose, turned his back to them, and walked to his horse as he answered:

"What do you mean, 'did *I* shoot him?' He's *still alive,* ain't he?"

CHAPTER 25

Alone together, Porter and Joseph arrived at the island's eastern shore. They approached a rowboat Porter had borrowed from former neighbor Anson Call. Across the river Porter could see his horse still hitched to a tree.

Neither could speak as they pushed the boat into the water. That accomplished, Porter glanced back at Joseph, whom he could discern in the moonlight had eyes glistening with tears. Porter was about to say, "We've come a long ways since Manchester, eh?" but couldn't get it out, when Joseph said:

"We've come a long way . . . "

"Since Manchester," finished Porter.

Both men smiled, although they could not talk further. Finally, Joseph stepped forward and hugged him. When they pulled away, Porter climbed into the boat and Joseph cleared his throat:

"Thanks for being a friend I know will be there till I die."

Porter stared at him. "Let's don't talk about dying."

Joseph continued, "You're a true brother." Joseph then cleared his throat. He added with difficulty, "Your loyalty is undeviating."

"I don't think so."

Joseph gazed at him curiously.

"When I was in Missouri, about to come back here to warn you of bounty hunters, I turned my horse around and went back to get my family."

"I remember those bounty-hunters," said Joseph. "They were the first." He smiled. "They weren't the brightest fellows, poor chaps, and we took care of them. Shadrach Roundy disarmed them and sent them home madder than hornets.

"Maybe you don't understand," said Porter. "I let that happen. I betrayed you."

"I don't think so."

"It's what happened."

"No," said Joseph. "You did the right thing."

"Choosing . . . "

"Your family?" said Joseph. "Certainly. They were in dangerous territory. You had to go. Porter, you're still the most trustworthy of men."

Porter felt relieved, having dreaded this confession for weeks. He smiled painfully as he sat down in the row boat, but finally said, "You'll keep an eye on my children?"

Joseph nodded.

As Porter began rowing away, Joseph studied him. He could read his soul, and perceive the weaknesses that Porter would someday recognize. He also knew his friend would correct them as best he could, but first had a few lessons in life to learn along the way. He could see the very core of Porter's soul, and what he viewed was a man who tried, by living according to the understanding and light he did possess. Joseph felt grateful there were such men. He wasn't asking for perfect men, only those who tried. Despite their drawbacks.

Joseph finally said:

"I'm sorry what you're having to go through."

"What're you talking about?"

"The sacrifices," said Joseph.

"Naw . . . it's a cheap price," said Porter. "But I just hope to have my family again."

Joseph had no response.

"Even if I don't," added Porter after a moment, "it'll still be a cheap price — and for helping to protect it a little, won't it?"

Joseph nodded, his throat tighter.

"Wasn't it you, Joseph, who said 'the Lord is forging servants for him, and the brighter the fire, the greater the opportunity?' So bring it on!" Porter laughed with anguish. For a moment he envisioned his private war before him, and kept rowing.

"The city's not the same anymore, is it?" spat out Joseph with a smile, wanting to change the subject so he could hold his composure. "Not with all these crazy bounty-hunters running around?"

"I reckon not," muttered Porter. "But maybe they'll be like wasps, buzzing just for a season, till they disappear."

"Porter, when that season has ended, we'll write. Then you can return."

Porter gazed emptily at him.

"I've thanked you before, and I must again," said Joseph. "Thank you for protecting me whenever I've needed you. My thanks goes far deeper than what you can understand."

Porter merely continued rowing. Half way across the river he noticed Joseph still standing on the island shore, staring. His boat then approached a patch of fog. He gave Joseph a short salute across the water, then disappeared.

Joseph stared into the fog, a tear glistening down his face. He thought a moment, and finally muttered aloud, "How I love that man."

A
PHOTOGRAPHIC ESSAY
OF NAUVOO, ILLINOIS

PART I

Photos by Richard Lloyd Dewey

Introduction to
Nauvoo Photographic Essay

This visual essay was photographed by the author September 23 - 25, 2000. Nauvoo's significance to Porter Rockwell is obvious to those who read Volumes 2 and 3 of the *Porter Rockwell Chronicles*. Porter's love for the city, his defense of Joseph Smith, and his integral tie to all the major events of the city's history in large part tell a significant portion of his own story.

The reader may journey through its fields and roads, and see the homes and city buildings that were part and parcel to Porter's and his friends' daily lives. Especially after visiting Nauvoo, to which the reader is strongly encouraged, one may feel the sense of wonder that inhabitants and visitors alike must have felt for so remarkable a town in its day, keeping in mind that just prior to migrating to this land they had resided in small log cabins and lean-to's along muddy streets in disorganized frontier towns. One may indeed wonder at the contrast between those structures of Porter's and Brigham's and Joseph's previous homes in New York, Ohio, Missouri, and Quincy, Illinois — including the ragtag huts in which they dwelled in some cases — to the substantial structures they built in this sprawling, magnificent "city on a hill" that had no equal from 1839 - 1846, the years in which Porter's people resided there.

The reader may, through the following pages, see the daily shops that Porter saw — from a local shoemaker, bakery, post office, and several general mercantiles to the nearest blacksmith and gunsmith shops down the street from Porter's residence — to even the Cultural Hall where both Porter and Brigham Young participated as actors in a local theater production. At the end of the essay is the temple that so many sacrificed for, in its incomplete state during reconstruction, which must eerily resemble the sight that for years lay before Nauvoo's thousands as it was slowly constructed on the hill.

The Preface to this volume details a brief history of Nauvoo. A study of the following photographs and captions will take the reader on a tour of perhaps the most fascinating city in North America, given its quick rise and demise, and the sacrifice that went into it, and especially the almost surreal elements of its opposition from within and without against which Porter boldly stood, which helped define his character as portrayed in this historical novel series.

In summary, Nauvoo had 350 brick homes, 650 frame houses, and 1,500 log houses, with 4,000 addtional outbuildings. A third of the structures were farms outside the residential section. Joseph planned out the city with large plots of land for residences, wide streets and sidewalks, with farms located away from the residential area to give the city's inhabitants a stronger, more cohesive feel of community. The city was far ahead of its time. Tradesmen and craftsmen from all over Europe who converted to the fold supplied all the city's needs — from clothes to equipment to services — making Nauvoo a complete, self-reliant, booming community.

Part I of the photo essay covers approximately half the 50 buildings remaining in Nauvoo of its original 2,500 structures that once existed. This photographic section documents for the reader the buildings and lands preserved so nobly by both the Church of Jesus Christ of Latter-day Saints and the Re-organized Church of Jesus Christ of Latter-day Saints. Not shown are the visitor centers of both groups which welcome thousands of visitors annually, because the purpose of this essay is to help the reader visually discover Porter's world as it existed then, during those remarkable seven years of his life, which furthered his character development for his remaining years.

Part II of this photographic essay of Nauvoo — which will be in Vol. 3 of the *Chronicles* — will conclude this tour of the city, and will primarily focus on exterior shots of all the remaining buildings in the city from Porter's era which are today under commercial and residential ownership.

Joseph Smith Homestead

This was the first home of the Prophet Joseph Smith,
the first President of the Church of Jesus Christ of Latter-day Saints,
in Nauvoo. The small cabin to the right was the original structure,
originally owned by James White, who was the first permanent settler
of Venus, Illinois, which became Commerce, later
renamed Nauvoo by the Mormons.

Above: Views of Joseph Smith Homestead (left to right:
from northeast, from east, from southeast, and from southwest).
Background: Mississippi River, as seen from Joseph Smith Homestead.

Above: Views of Joseph Smith Homestead
(left to right: from west, closer view of cabin from west, closeup of
cabin from north, and Homestead from north).

Background: Mississippi River, as seen from
Joseph Smith homestead, looking south.

Above: Joseph Smith homestead as seen from northwest, showing Nauvoo House in background (closest to homestead).

Below: Well at Joseph Smith homestead.

Top: Joseph Smith homestead from east. Mississippi River is behind trees.

Inset: Outhouse at Joseph Smith homestead.

Bottom: Burial site of Joseph Smith, his brother Hyrum, and his wife Emma, at southwest corner of Joseph Smith homestead.

Joseph Smith Mansion House

Built in 1842-1843, the Mansion House is located a block
northeast of the Joseph Smith homestead.

Top: View from a distance, from west.
Bottom left and right: From northwest.

View of Joseph
Smith Mansion
House from
southwest.

From south-
southwest.

From east.

Joseph Smith's Red Brick Store

Three views of store located near Joseph Smith homestead.
Mississippi river is visible in background.

Nauvoo House

Two views of the Nauvoo House, which served as the premier hotel for visitors to Nauvoo. Above: view from southeast. Below: view from southwest.

Nauvoo House, seen from northwest.

Top inset: Rear of Nauvoo House, seen from northeast.
Bottom inset: Back of Nauvoo house, seen from east.
Mississippi River is in background.

Seventies Hall

View from the south. The Seventies were a priesthood organization assigned
to missionary work. This hall was built in 1843-1844 under the direction of
Brigham Young, then president of the Quorum of the Twelve Apostles, as a
meeting place and training center for Nauvoo's 15 quorums of Seventies,
to improve their effectiveness as teachers. The main floor was used for chapel
worship services, lectures, and classes. The second floor held a city library, art
exhibits, a museum, and office space for the Seventies.

Pulpit and benches on main floor of Seventies Hall.

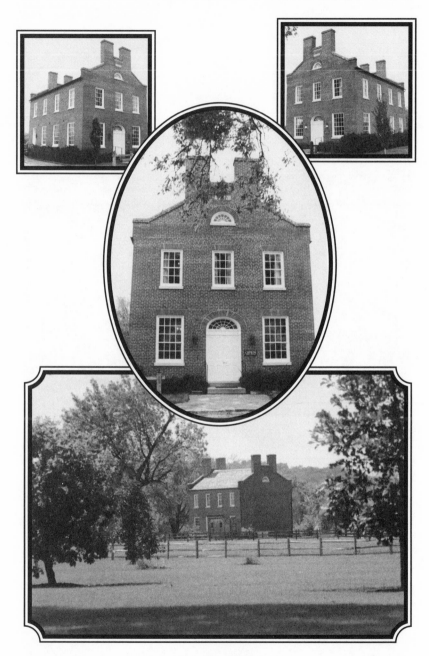

Seventies Hall.

Interior views, upstairs, Seventies Hall.

Seventies Hall as seen from Brigham Young home.
Inset: View of Seventies Hall as seen from east.

Top: Staircase leading to second floor of Seventies Hall.
Center: Seventies Hall as seen from northeast.
Bottom: Heating stove in Seventies Hall.

Seventies Hall as seen from northeast, near Brigham Young home.

View of Seventies Hall from east.

Cultural Hall

Begun in 1842 and dedicated in 1844, the Cultural Hall was a multi-purpose meeting hall. Plays, concerts, recitals, receptions, parties, dances, art shows, church services, and funerals all took place here. In addition, it was used as a meeting place for Masons, the Nauvoo Legion (the town militia), the police department, and the city planning commission. At one time it was also used as a grainery. The Mormons last used it as a place for manufacturing wagon boxes for the westward migration. Contractor for its construction was Lucius Scovil, a baker. It was sold in a sheriff's sale in 1851 for $4.47.

Views of Cultural Hall.
Above: View from northeast.
Left photos below show views from northwest.
Right photos below show views from southwest.

Seats in Cultural Hall. Pine benches were painted to look like oak. Pine pillars were painted to look like marble, and polished with beeswax for shine.

Stage of the Cultural Hall. The hall held about 100 theatergoers.

The playbill for *Pizarro*, the first play performed in the Cultural Hall, 19 days after the dedication of the building, Brigham Young played the part of the High Priest.

Third floor of the Cultural Hall, looking from the east.

Top floor of Cultural Hall, showing floor on which Joseph Smith chalked out plans for the trek to the Great Basin. View is from the west.

Dumbwaiter in northwest corner of Cultural Hall.

Outhouse for the Cultural Hall.

Original foundations of Cultural Hall, made of limestone and brick.

The outhouse was a two-seater.

Cultural Hall southeast basement entrance.

Agricultural lands behind the Cultural Hall.

Limestone quarry from which stone was taken
for construction of the Nauvoo Temple.

Printing Office / Post Office Complex

Built by James Ivins, a convert from Toms River, New Jersey, this complex consisted of a home flanked by two commercial buildings. It was built probably in 1843. The Printing Office moved in to the building on the left in 1845, and John Taylor, who served as editor and publisher, lived in the home in the center.

Printing Office

Here was printed the periodical the *Times and Seasons*, as well as two weekly newspapers, the *Nauvoo Neighbor* and the *Nauvoo Wasp*. Other Church literature was also published here, in addition to commercial and private printing.

Fonts and type composition equipment in the Printing Office.

Facade of the Printing Office.

Presses from the era are housed in the Printing Office.

Printing Office and a copy of the *Nauvoo Neighbor*.

Post Office

View of the Post Office from the northeast. General merchandise, books, and stationery were also sold in the same building.

Three types of letters used for correspondence: postage paid, postage due, and "sad" letters (identified by black border) announcing deaths and other tragedies.

In order to save paper, correspondents frequently wrote letters like this, with criss-crossed writing covering each sheet.

View of mercantile section in the Post Office building.

Merchandise available for sale in the Post Office building.

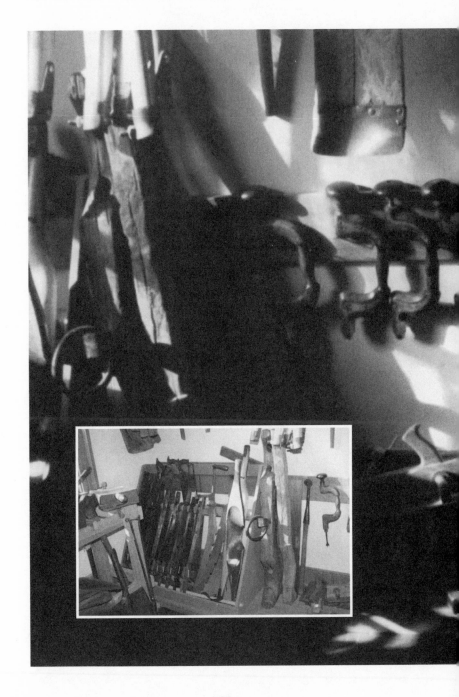

Merchandise in Post Office building.

Stovepipe and merchandise in Post Office building.

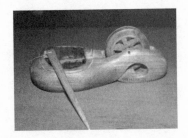

Ceramic canteen.   Berry juicer.

John Taylor Home

The Federalist-style residence sandwiched between the Printing Office and the Post Office was home to John Taylor for a short time. John Taylor later became the third President of the Church of Jesus Christ of Latter-day Saints.

Dining room.

John Taylor residence.

Above: Rocking horse in John Taylor home. The rocking horse had to be left behind when the family fled Nauvoo. John Taylor's young son cried about it for days as they made their journey into Iowa. Distressed by his son's grief, John Taylor rode all the way back to Nauvoo to fetch the horse. The family tied it to the side of the wagon for the trek to the Great Basin. The rocking horse is about 18" tall.

Interiors of John Taylor residence.

Bedrooms.

John Taylor home.
Bottom photo shows a shaving stand.

Sylvester Stoddard Tin Shop

Stoddard's tin shop, completed in 1844, was located just north of the Post Office. He made and sold a wide variety of tinware. He also made and installed stovepipes, including at the Mansion House and Hyrum Smith's home. View above is from the northeast; below, from the southeast.

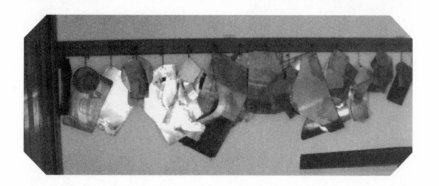

Tin, tools, equipment, and finished tinware in Stoddard tin shop.

Stoddard's tin shop
also served as a residence.

Cupboards, table, and stove
in Stoddard tin shop.

Stoddard tin shop as seen from northeast.

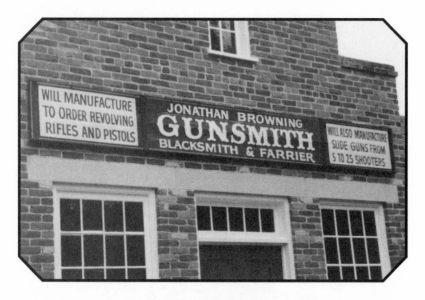

Jonathan Browning Gunsmith Shop

Facade of Jonathan Browning's gunsmith shop. Jonathan Browning invented
one of the earliest repeating rifles.

Jonathan Browning gunsmith shop as seen from west.
Browning's home was attached to the shop.

Gun-making equipment in Browning gunsmith shop.

Bellows

Forge

Grinding wheel

Anvil

Guns and gun-making tools in Browning gunsmith shop.

Jonathan Browning, a native of Kentucky, became a blacksmith in his youth, then later focused on gunsmithing. He converted to the Mormon religion near Quincy, Illinois, 43 miles south of Nauvoo. He moved his shop to Nauvoo in 1843, where he lived in a two-room log cabin on this site. By 1845 he completed this two-story house, with a well, cellar, kitchen, and one-story extension for blacksmithing, metal working, and gunsmithing.

Exterior shots of Browning gunsmith shop and home.
Top two shots show view from southwest.
Bottom shot is of well located to the south of the building.

Browning home.

Jonathan Browning made about 400 guns
in Kentucky, Illinois, Iowa, and Utah. His son, John Moses Browning,
worked at his father's gunsmith shop in Ogden, Utah, and became famous
for inventing the automatic machine gun.

Webb Bros. Blacksmith & Wagon Shop

The Webb brothers stayed to the end in 1846, building wagons for
the westward migration. Five brothers worked at the craft.
Views from southeast (above) and southwest (below).

Interior shots of Webb Bros.
blacksmith shop.

Ox yoke in blacksmith shop.

Ox and mule shoes, displaying the versatility of the blacksmiths.

Neck yoke for horses (above) and "double tree" (below), in blacksmith shop.

Hobbles used on horses' front feet so they wouldn't stray. Indians could not figure out how to take them off, so they couldn't steal the horses.

"Double tree" in Webb Bros.
wainwright shop.

Interior of wainwright shop.

"One size fits all" does not describe horseshoes.
Many think of the Clydesdale (far left) as the world's largest horse. Notice that
the Clydesdale's shoe is dwarfed by the Shire's shoe (far right). In the center
is a shoe for a typical riding horse.

Wood-carving bench
in wainwright shop.

Wheel, spokes, and fellow.

Lathe in Webb Bros. wainwright shop.

Equipment used to bend wheel rims.

Axe sharpener.

Above: Sign outside Webb Bros. wainwright shop,
where they assembled wagons.
Below: Completed wagon inside wainwright shop.

Samples of the Webb Bros.' craft, outside their wainwright shop.

Barn and outhouse behind Webb
Bros. shops.

Well behind Webb Bros.
wainwright shop.

Seventies Hall, framed by porch on back of Webb blacksmith shop.

Riser Home and Boot Shop

Riser was one of 12 shoemakers in Nauvoo. His marketing angle was that he made shoes at the cheapest price. He employed four assistants who worked in the shop which was in his small home. The property on which Riser's shop was built was 200 feet deep, but only 16 feet wide! Riser built the house to the full width of the property.

Top: Riser boot shop as seen from southeast. Center: Well behind Riser boot shop. Bottom: View of Riser's property from southwest.

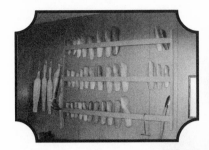

Interior of Riser Boot Shop, showing shoe-making equipment and tools.
Riser's family lived upstairs, and would come downstairs to the shop at night,
where the cooking was done.

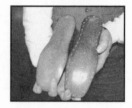

Demonstration of processes used in the construction of shoes.
Wooden pegs and thread were used.

Left and right shoes were a luxury. Most shoes were square-toed
and designed to fit either foot. The wearer could gain an extra
50% to 60% of wear by switching feet.

Scovil Bakery

Lucius Scovil's bakery was located next to the Cultural Hall. Shown here are the main bakehouse, summer bakehouse, and well, as seen from the north.

Main bakehouse at Scovil
Bakery, seen from northeast.

Scovil Bakery summer
bakehouse, seen from northwest.

Scovil main bakehouse,
seen from southwest.

View from northwest of Scovil Bakery.
The bakery had two indoor ovens which were partially buried to retain heat.

Ovens in summer bakehouse.　　　　Interior of Scovil Bakery.

Scovil Bakery summer bakehouse, seen from northeast.

Cabinet in Scovil Bakery.

Outhouse behind Scovil Bakery complex, view from west.

Closeup showing baking
implements.

Interior of main bakehouse,
Scovil Bakery.

Lucius Scovil was contractor for the Cultural Hall.
He also managed a catering service. From the bakery
he sold not only bread, but also cakes, crackers,
candies, and jellies.

Closeup of well at Scovil Bakery.

Interior of main bakehouse.

Ovens of main bakehouse,
Scovil Bakery.

Stairs leading to basement of main bakehouse,
showing limestone foundation.

Lyon Drug & Variety Store

This view from the southwest shows the store and attached house.
Lyon opened his store in 1840 in a log cabin on the same block. The
large, brick store was completed in 1843, selling medicines,
household items, hardware, textiles, boots and shoes, books,
stationery, produce, and crockery.

Lyon Drug Store, as seen from northwest.

Views of Lyon Drug Store from northeast (above left and below),
and from southwest.

Views of outbuilding associated with Lyon Drug Store.

Scales inside drugstore. Note the
distorted view of the outside
produced by the old window glass.

Herbs and tonics for sale in
drugstore.

Medicines.

Herbs.

View out window of drugstore.

Items for sale.

Spices.

Soaps.

Ivory toothbrushes in Lyon drugstore.

Herbs for sale.

Various items for sale.

Additional herbs.

Serving ware for sale in drugstore. Top shelf: Copper lustre. Second shelf: Apple ware. Third & fourth shelves: Transfer ware.

Lower photo: Brooms for sale.

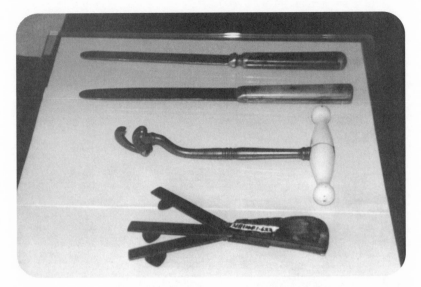

Utensils typical of those sold in drugstore.

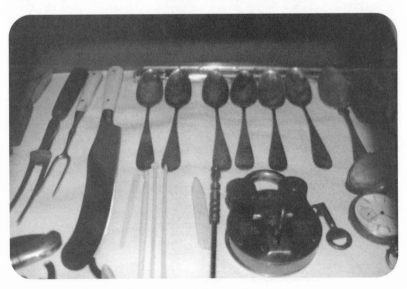

Silverware and padlock.

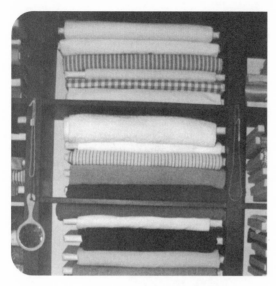

Bolts of fabric.

Bear skin and knitted goods.

Leather canteen, map canister, and
men's leather effects bag.

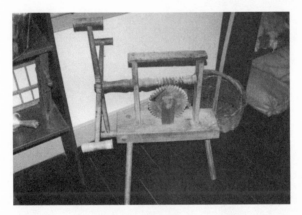

Spinning wheel for sale.

Glassware.

Ribbons, thread, knitting needles, and
crochet hooks in drugstore.

Guns on display.

Sundry goods.

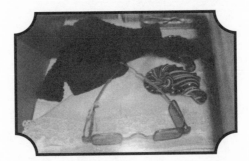

Rare sunglasses.

Slide rule and telescope.

Pewter ware. The boxes were used to capture and tag bees by dusting their wings with flour to make them more visible, in order to discover the hives from which they came.

Beehives, smoked hams, and turkeys.

Bartered goods in Lyon Drug Store, including beehive, far right.

Barrels of assorted foods.

Kegs of product.

Workman/Field cabin (foreground), Patti Sessions cabin, and Lyon drugstore.

Patti Sessions cabin in foreground, Lyon drugstore in background,
seen from east.

Chicken coop and outhouse for Patti
sessions cabin.

Well at Patti Sessions cabin, with outhouse
and chicken coop showing in background.

Patti Sessions Cabin

Patti was mother-in-law of Mr. Lyons of the drugstore.
This view is from the northeast.

Patti Sessions cabin and well, seen from northeast.

Interior of Patti Sessions cabin. Hearth and table.

Birdhouse at Patti Sessions cabin.

Bed in Patti Sessions cabin.

Workman/Field Cabin

The Workman/Field cabin was directly east of Patti Sessions cabin.
Shown here as seen from northwest.

Workman/Field cabin as seen from southeast.

Replicas of log cabins
from Nauvoo era.

Pendleton Log Home and School

Of the 2,500 homes in Nauvoo, more than 1,400 were log homes. This one, built in 1843, was the home of Dr. Calvin Crane Pendleton and his family. Pendleton was an herbal doctor, gunsmith, and school teacher who also set broken bones. He taught reading, writing, and arithmetic to children, and penmanship to adults. This view is from the southwest.

View from the south of Pendleton log home and school.

Lower left, and center: Calvin Pendleton
log home and school as seen from southeast.
Upper right: View from the east.

Interior shots of Pendleton log home.

More interiors of Pendleton log home.

Herbs hung out to dry.
The Pendletons grew and processed herbs
for medicinal purposes.

Commode in Pendleton log house.

Interior of Pendleton school, showing all three of the benches for pupils.

Teacher's lectern in Pendleton log school.

Property owned by Porter Rockwell and his father, Orin,
at the north end of Nauvoo

THIS PROPERTY BELONGED TO
PORTER ROCKWELL

ONE OF THE COLORFUL FIGURES
OF THE MORMON PIONEER ERA

BORN JUNE 28 1813   DIED JUNE 9 1878

SELF APPOINTED BODY GUARD FOR
JOSEPH SMITH

SERVED FOR YEARS AS SHERIFF & MARSHAL
IN SALT LAKE COUNTY AND KEPT A MAIL
STATION NEAR POINT OF THE MOUNTAIN
WHERE UTAH STATE PRISON NOW STANDS

HE RISKED HIS LIFE MANY TIMES IN
DEFENSE OF THE CHURCH LEADERS

HE JOINED THE CHURCH IN 1830
THE SAME YEAR IT WAS ORGANIZED

Site of Porter Rockwell property at
intersection of Munson and Partridge streets,
with commemorative marker.

Brickyard Replica

Nauvoo had 7 brickyards. Two were on the flats and five were up on the bluff, where the clay pits were located to make brick. 4 million bricks per year were manufactured in Nauvoo, just enough to cover the amount needed to build the 350 brick homes in the city. Of the 50 remaining original homes in Nauvoo, 41 are made of brick, 8 are frame houses, and one is a log cabin.

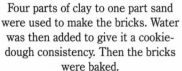

Four parts of clay to one part sand were used to make the bricks. Water was then added to give it a cookie-dough consistency. Then the bricks were baked.

Above: Replica of brick kiln at Nauvoo. The actual kilns were larger than this. Facing page: Brick-making facilities and equipment.

Brick-making facilities at brickyard.

Piles of bricks at brickyard..

Building directly north of Nauvoo House.

South wing of an early hotel.

William Gheen Home

William Marks Home

Marks, an eventual enemy, was a close neighbor of Joseph Smith. The Marks home is about a block from the Joseph Smith Homestead and from the Mansion House, as well. This view is from the south.

William Marks home as seen from southwest.

George Laub Home

The George Laub home is located on Parley Street.

Aaron Johnson Home

Views from southwest, south, and southeast.

Simeon Adams Dunn home

Hiram Clark Home

Home from Joseph Smith era, at north end of Nauvoo.
Now a private residence.

Henry Thomas Home

Henry Thomas Home

Vinson Knight Home

Home immediately west of Aaron Johnson home, as seen from south.

Same home, seen from southwest.

Snow/Ashby Duplex

View from northeast.

Snow / Ashby duplex as seen from the east.

Snow / Ashby duplex as seen from the southeast.

Orson Hyde Home

Top: View from southeast.
Center: Orson Hyde barn.
Bottom: Home, from northeast.

David D. Yearsley Home

View from southeast.

From east.

**Jacob Weiler
Home**

From northeast.

William Weeks Home

William Weeks was the architect of the Nauvoo Temple and other major buildings—the Cultural Hall, Nauvoo House, and Arsenal.

Winslow Farr Home

Samuel Williams Home

Sidney Rigdon Home

Background: View from north.
Top inset: From west.
Bottom inset: From southwest.

Sarah Granger Kimball House & Barn

In 1840 Sarah and her husband, Hiram Kimball, moved to this frame house, which had already been built. Sarah organized women to make shirts for workers on the Nauvoo temple.

Sarah Granger Kimball Home

View from south.

From northwest.

Sarah Granger Kimball Home

Sarah Granger Kimball Home

Interior of Sarah Granger Kimball home.

Sarah Granger Kimball home, ground floor.

Sarah Granger Kimball Home

Interior, second floor.

Interior, second floor.

Interior, ground floor.

Second floor of Sarah Granger Kimball home.

More of second floor.

Field south of Sarah Granger Kimball farm.

Sarah Granger Kimball home.

Sarah Granger Kimball barn.

Sarah
Granger
Kimball
barn.

Fields and barn behind Sarah Granger Kimball home.

Brigham Young Home

Brigham Young, the great American colonizer who led the Mormons west to Utah, was the second president of the LDS Church. Meetings of presiding councils of the church were held in the east wing of this home, which was built in 1843-1844. View above is from northeast; below, from northwest.

Back of Brigham Young home, as seen from west.

View from behind, from southwest.

Another view from southwest.

Outhouse behind Brigham Young home.

Brigham Young home as seen from northeast.

Shed behind Brigham Young home.

Chauncey Webb Home

Webb, the blacksmith and wainwright, lived in this home,
which is directly north of the blacksmith shop.
View above is from northeast,
below is from southeast.

Chauncey Webb home, as seen from the east.

Stables north of the Chauncey Webb home.

Fences on Chauncey Webb property.

Westward view from behind Chauncey Webb home.

Back yard of Chauncey Webb home.

Lucy Mack Smith Home

This home was built in 1843 by Joseph Noble, a justice of the peace, who moved with his wife Mary to Nauvoo in 1839. The LDS church bought it in the spring of 1846, before the migration, and gave it to Joseph Smith's mother, Lucy Mack Smith. She planned to go west after the Utah settlement was established, but died in illness.

View above is from the northeast.

Lucy Mack Smith home, as seen from southeast.

Lucy Mack Smith home, as seen from northeast.

Well, east of
Lucy Mack Smith
home.

Cellar.

Back yard.

Facing page, and above: Interior views of Lucy Mack Smith home.

Lucy Mack Smith home.

A nearly complete set of stoneware owned by the Smith family,
located in the Lucy Mack Smith home, is among the very few
surviving Smith family heirlooms.

Joseph W. Coolidge Home

Joseph Coolidge was a cabinet maker and master builder. His skills are seen in the Mansion House and other Nauvoo buildings. Shown above is his home, which was built in 1843, in a view from the southeast. Below is a view of the gardens surrounding the house.

Joseph W. Coolidge home, as seen from northeast.

Gardens at Joseph W. Coolidge home.

German inscriptions on Joseph W. Coolidge home.
Top fully visible line reads: "This house is mine, and yet not mine.
So will it be with whoever follows me." Second line reads: "I was here.
Whoever reads this was here, too."

Cellar to Joseph W. Coolidge home.

Pump outside Joseph W. Coolidge home.

This fireplace in Joseph W. Coolidge home was discovered behind a wall after the LDS Church bought the home in the early 1970s.

Armoire in Coolidge home, shown both open and shut,
utilized an interesting method to hang clothes.

The oven in the Coolidge home was the largest in Nauvoo.
Eighteen loaves of bread could be baked simultaneously.

Pottery-making display in Coolidge home.

Barrel-making display in Coolidge home.

Candle-making display.

Wilford Woodruff Home

Wilford Woodruff became the fourth president of the Church of Jesus Christ of Latter-day Saints. Wilford Woodruff built his own house. He bartered for 1500 bricks, using a pair of shoes, a pair of pantaloons, and a shawl, worth $7.84. But after laying four rows of brick he found them to be of inferior quality, and decided to pick his own brick from then on. He was very picky in choosing his bricks. This is the best surviving of the Federal style homes in Nauvoo.

The view here is from the northeast.

Wilford Woodruff managed the Nauvoo House Provision Store, which disbursed supplies to those who worked on the Nauvoo House. He later became the business manager of the Church Printing Office. He began building this house upon returning from a mission to England in 1841. By summer 1844, the family moved into the house. Less than two years later they abandoned it for the trek west. This is the first building in Nauvoo to have a documented and authentic architectural restoration.

Well and outhouse behind Wilford Woodruff home.

Because he complained of always being cold,
Wilford had a fireplace in every room.

Child's room in Woodruff home.

Bedroom upstairs in Woodruff home. Wilford's wife Phoebe made the quilt.

Wilford Woodruff's hat box.
While on his mission, Wilford would sit on it at train stations, waiting for
trains, and stand on it at street corners, preaching.
Obviously, it was sturdily built.

His and Her chairs and footstools in Woodruff home.
Phoebe's is on the left.

A pair of spinning wheels in Wilford Woodruff home.

Cooking utensils.

Picture of tiger on wall in downstairs parlor of Woodruff home
is crewel stitched.

Desk in Woodruff home. The glasses, glasses case,
paperweights, and inkwell were all
Wilford's own.

Dining room in Woodruff home.
The silverware was obtained from two trips to England.

Cabinet, Wilford Woodruff home.

Heber C. Kimball Home

Heber was a blacksmith and potter, who became one of the first Apostles in 1835. The Kimballs moved to Nauvoo in 1839. After a two-year mission to the British Isles, Heber returned to the United States and lived in a small log-and-brick house on this site before building this home. He completed the west two-story section (the larger one to the left, as seen in this southeast view) in 1845. He and his family were only able to enjoy living in the home for a few months before they had to leave it in the exodus of the Saints from Nauvoo.

Heber C. Kimball home, as seen from northwest.

Heber C. Kimball home, as seen from west.

Upstairs front of Heber C. Kimball home.

Exterior of Heber C. Kimball home, as seen from southwest.

Architectural details on Heber C. Kimball home.

View of Heber C. Kimball home from northwest,
showing pump behind the house.

Interior views of Heber C. Kimball home.

Parlor.

Piano in Kimball home; 1808 Broadwood—same model used by Beethoven
in composing several symphonies.

Dining room in Heber C. Kimball home.
The fine china plates are from England. Included in the home is a china plate
depicting the Nauvoo Temple. In 1846, 1,800 such plates were
commissioned by the baker, Scovil. Only 20 remain today.

Kimball home interior. The table is a Chippendale.
Heber shopped all over Europe for furniture.

Staircase in Kimball home.

Grandfather clock
upstairs in Kimball home,
from Dundee, Scotland.

Cabinet

Nursery in Kimball home.

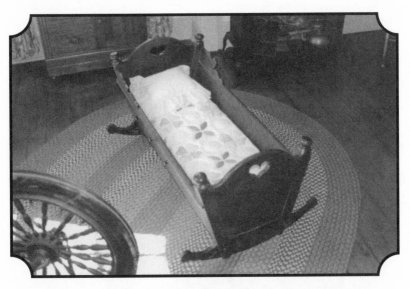

Cradle in Kimball home. Ropes were stretched across the top of the crib and tied at the knobs to form a safety harness, so that the baby did not fall out when the cradle rocked.

Pre-1800 spinning wheel in Kimball home.

437

Stereoscope in music room of Kimball home worked like a modern
Viewmaster, but used motion picture images. Young women
would entertain their beaus with this apparatus.

"Sparking" lamps in Kimball home. Sparking was a term used for kissing.
When the lamps burned out, it was time for a suitor to go home.
If a young woman's father liked a certain young man, he would put
more oil in the lamps at the beginning of the evening.

Stove in Kimball home. The umbrella-shaped object on top of the stove, under the stovepipe, is a humidifier.

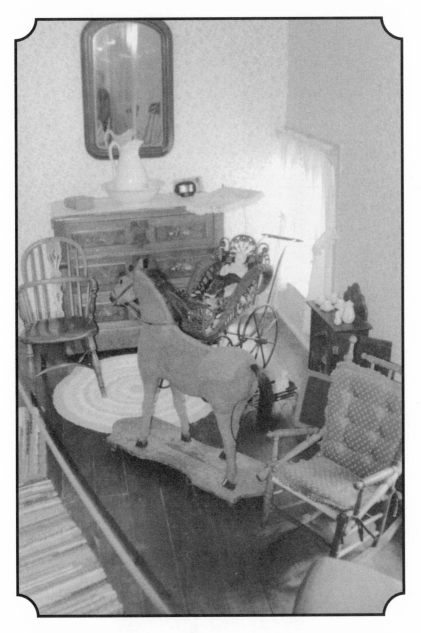

Toy room.

Music box in Kimball home created beautiful music.
Discs for playing different tunes were stacked below the box.

Condition of the interior of the Kimball home before restoration.
A previous owner requested that one room be left as is.

Ferry Landing at End of Parley Street

The Saints launched westward across the Mississippi River from here. Horse-powered flatboats and a steamboat, the *Maid of Iowa*, operated here between 1839 and 1846. Between 1847 and 1868, 80,000 Latter-day Saints migrated west to Utah before the building of the Transcontinental Railroad. They made the migration in 230 wagon trains and 10 handcart companies. Thousands died en route.

Sunstone from Nauvoo Temple.

The last view the Saints had of Nauvoo
as they launched across the Mississippi.

Adjacent to the LDS Visitors Center in Nauvoo is the garden known as the
Monument to Women. This statue, depicting Joseph Smith giving Emma a coin
to start the Female Relief Society—forerunner of today's Relief Society—
is located in the garden.

Views of author's favorite statue in the garden.

Mississippi River seen from
north section of Nauvoo.

Nauvoo temple reconstruction underway, September 2000.

Nauvoo, Illinois, mid-1840s
by Dan Thornton

Art prints of *Nauvoo, Illinois, mid-1840s*, depicted on the front and rear of this book's dust jacket, are available from the publisher.

- **Limited Edition**
  signed and numbered, large size (28.5"w x 19"h)
  $135.00 plus shipping & handling ($15.00, plus
  $1.00 for each additional print sent to same address)

- **Artist's Proof**
  (same size)
  $200.00 plus shipping & handling ($15.00, plus
  $1.00 for each additional print sent to same address)

- **Greeting Card Packs**
  unsigned, 10 cards and envelopes
  $25.00 plus shipping & handling ($3.00, plus
  $1.00 for each additional pack sent to same address)

As the 860 Limited Edition art prints sell out, the collectors' value may substantially increase. Nearly half are sold as of December 1, 2000.

Send check or money order to:
Stratford Books, P.O. Box 1371, Provo, Utah 84603-1371
Utah residents, add 6.25% sales tax .

453

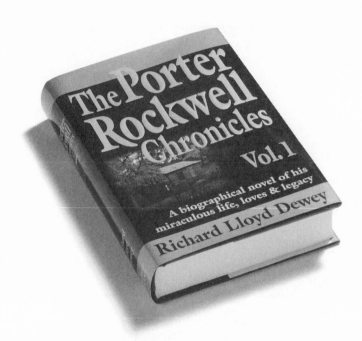

The Porter Rockwell Chronicles, Vol. 1
by Richard Lloyd Dewey

Hardcover, $23.88 (Reg. $27.50)   ISBN: 0-9616024-6-5

Read the story of Porter Rockwell in this initial volume of the exciting, new biographical novel series.

This first volume details Rockwell's formative years as a teenage protector of a peaceful religious community; his close friendship with Joseph Smith; his engaging yet humorous courtship with Luana Beebe; and the persecutions which eventually killed his father. From these events, Porter would later become Brigham Young's bodyguard and the most productive U.S. Marshal in American history, killing more outlaws than Wyatt Earp, Doc Holladay, Tom Horn, and Batt Masterson ... *combined*.

Reading this book allows the reader to see what a real hero is — including his rough edges. Noted British journalist Jules Remy wrote of Rockwell in 1861: "He is the stuff from which heroes are wrought. It is he who is ever at hand where there is a sacrifice to be made which can be of advantage to the oppressed."

Look for it in your favorite bookstore,
or to obtain autographed copies, see last page.

Porter Rockwell: A Biography
by Richard Lloyd Dewey

Hardcover, $22.95   ISBN: 0-9616024-0-6

The epic biography that traces Porter Rockwell from turbulent Eastern beginnings to battles with Midwestern mobs to extraordinary gunfights on the American frontier. Quotes hundreds of journals, letters, and court records. Illustrated by western artist, Clark Kelley Price.

**Look for it in your favorite bookstore,
or to obtain autographed copies, see last page.**

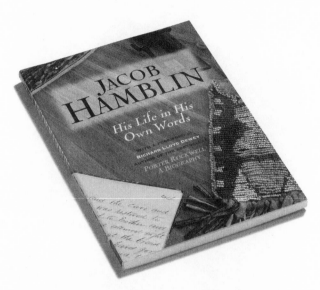

Jacob Hamblin: His Life in His Own Words
Foreword by Richard Lloyd Dewey

Softcover, $10.95   ISBN: 0-9616024-5-7

Far from the gun-toting reputation of super-lawman Porter Rockwell, Jacob Hamblin was known in early Western history as the supreme peacemaker.

No less exciting than Porter's account, Jacob's adventures encountered apparent Divine intervention at every turn, a reward seemingly bestowed to certain souls given to absolute faith. And in his faith, like Porter, Jacob Hamblin was one of those incredibly rare warriors who was *absolutely fearless*.

His migrations from Ohio to Utah with life-and-death adventures at every turn keep the reader spellbound in this unabridged, autobiographical account of the Old West's most unusual adventurer among Native Americans.

In his own words, Jacob Hamblin bares his soul with no pretense, unveiling an eye-witness journal of pioneer attempts to co-exist peacefully with Native brothers, among whom he traveled unarmed, showing his faith in God that he would not be harmed.

Easily considered the most successful — and bravest — diplomat to venture into hostile territory single-handedly, Hamblin takes the reader into hearts of darkness and hearts of light.

**Look for it in your favorite bookstore,
or to obtain autographed copies, see last page.**

New Evidences of Christ in Ancient America
by Blaine M. Yorgason, Bruce W. Warren, and Harold Brown

Hardcover, $24.95   ISBN: 0-929753-01-1

In 1947 California lawyer Tom Ferguson threw a shovel over his shoulder and marched into the jungles of southern Mexico. Teamed with world-class scholar Bruce Warren, they found a *mountain* of evidence supporting *Book of Mormon* claims. Now the reader can follow their adventure as they unearth amazing archaeological discoveries and ancient writings, all of which shut the mouths of the critics who say such evidences do not exist. In this volume, the *newest* archaeological revidences are also presented.

Endorsed by Hugh Nibley.

**Look for it in your favorite bookstore,
or to obtain autographed copies, see last page.**

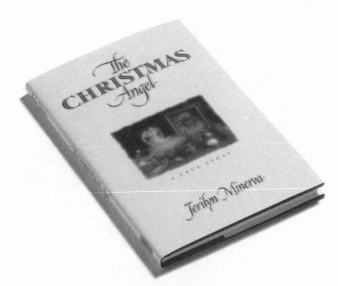

The Christmas Angel
A True Story
by Jerilyn Minerva

Hardcover, $12.99   ISBN: 0-929753-02-X

Here is the heart-warming — and at times heart-breaking — true story of Chrissy, a lovely, frail "throw-away child," and her odyssey spanning two Christmas seasons that brought her into the arms and heart of the author.

Helen Keller once said, "Although the world is full of suffering, it is also full of the overcoming of it." Chrissy's struggle to survive the first few years of her life is inspiring. "It's a miracle she lasted until we could find each other," says Jerilyn.

Share with Jerilyn the touching story of Chrissy's climbing of life's mountains, as she finds her way from God's arms to the author's, for a long-awaited reunion.

The Christmas Angel Audio Book Unabridged text of the book, read by the author. Two cassettes, approx. 2 hrs. total running time.

$15.95   ISBN: 0-929753-03-8

**Look for these in your favorite bookstore,
or to obtain copies by mail, see last page.**

How to Teach Your Children to Say "No" to Drugs (and Keep Their Friends)
by Leo Paur

Hardcover, $12.95   ISBN: 0-929753-00-3

For an adolescent, refusing drugs isn't as easy as just saying no. Refusal seems to take on greater proportions, as if saying no meant rejecting friendship, acceptance, individuality, or adulthood. Even kids from strong families — kids that are religiously active — have a hard time doing something they think will alienate their friends. Saying no is hard enough, but saying no and knowing how to confront the reaction that comes next . . . that's *really* hard.

This book helps parents develop within their children the strength to turn away from drugs and at the same time have a postive influence on their peers without alienation.

This inspiringly written book comes from first-hand experiences by a high school teacher who for eight years taught substance abuse prevention in California and was also a high school football coach skilled in working with adolescents.

It is an approach to drug education that gives parents the proven techniques they need to educate their children effectively in the home. And how to do so while their children are *young*, before drugs become a problem.

**Look for it in your favorite bookstore,
or to obtain autographed copies, see last page.**

Porter Rockwell Returns
by Clark Kelley Price

36"w x 24"h, $30.00   ISBN: 0-929753-0-6

This classic color print of the painting by renowned western artist Clark Kelley Price depicts Porter Rockwell coming home at night in a lightning storm through downtown Lehi, Utah.

In this vivid scene, Rockwell is returning from a hard day's work, with an outlaw draped over the horse he has in tow.

**Look for it in your favorite bookstore,
or to obtain by mail, see last page.**

Ordering Information

☛All books ordered by mail are autographed.

The Porter Rockwell Chronicles, Vol. 1   (Reg. $27.50) **$23.88**
by Richard Lloyd Dewey. Hardcover, 490 pp. ISBN: 0-9616024-6-5

The Porter Rockwell Chronicles, Vol. 2   (Reg. $27.50) **$23.88**
by Richard Lloyd Dewey. Hardcover, 452 pp. ISBN: 0-9616024-7-3

Porter Rockwell: A Biography   **$22.95**
by Richard Lloyd Dewey. Hardcover, 612 pp. ISBN: 0-9616024-0-6

Jacob Hamblin: His Life in His Own Words   **$10.95**
Foreword by Richard Lloyd Dewey. Softcover, 128 pp.
ISBN: 0-9616024-5-7

New Evidences of Christ in Ancient America   **$24.95**
by Blaine M. Yorgason, Bruce W. Warren, and Harold Brown
Hardcover, 442 pp. ISBN: 0-929753-01-1

The Christmas Angel: A True Story   **$12.99**
by Jerilyn Minerva. Hardcover, 71 pp. ISBN: 0-929753-02-X

The Christmas Angel Audio Book   **$15.95**
Unabridged, read by the author. Two cassettes, 2 hrs. approx.
running time. ISBN: 0-929753-02-X

How to Teach Your Children to Say "No" to Drugs   **$12.95**
(and Keep Their Friends)
by Leo Paur. Hardcover, 128 pp. ISBN: 0-929753-00-3

Porter Rockwell Returns Art Print   **$30.00**
by Clark Kelley Price. 36"w x 24"h, unsigned. ISBN: 0-929753-0-6

Utah residents, add 6.25% sales tax to price of items
(before shipping & handling).

Shipping & Handling:

For books and audio books, add $4.95 for first item and $1.00 for each
additional item sent to same address.

For *Porter Rockwell Returns* art prints, add $10.00 for first print and
$1.00 for each additional print sent to same address.

Send check or money order to:
Stratford Books
P.O. Box 1371, Provo, Utah 84603-1371

Prices subject to change.

461